Herbert Street

A Tale of Hemel Hempstead

David Satchel

A Bright Pen Book

Text Copyright © David Satchel 2011

Cover design by David Satchel ©

British Library Cataloguing Publication Data.
A catalogue record for this book is available from the British Library

ISBN 978-07552-1356-6

Authors OnLine Ltd
19 The Cinques
Gamlingay, Sandy
Bedfordshire SG19 3NU
England

This book is also available in e-book format, details of which are available at www.authorsonline.co.uk

To Ann Dean who would have loved this book.

James Snook and the Wicked Lady of Markyate Cell were real life highway robbers who committed their crimes in Hertfordshire and died in that county. All the other characters depicted in this novel are fictional and are not intended to resemble anyone living or dead.

The action in this story takes place
in Hemel Hempstead sometime in the future.

Chapter One

Exhumation

Despite the stinging sweat in his eyes and the late afternoon February gloom, Ben Carter could just see the end of his spade as it pierced the damp clay nearly two metres down at the bottom of the hole. He was enjoying working his sixty-year old lungs and muscles and encouraged himself with memories of school holidays –making dugouts large enough for a nine-year old boy and his friends to climb in and shoot air guns at imagined enemies and catapults at real ones. With a dull thud his spade hit what he hoped was the lid of a coffin. Moments later frantic scraping revealed what was indeed the corner of some sort of wooden box. "Found it!" he shouted and leant back against the side of the hole to get his breath, cursing gently as crumbs of loose soil fell down the back of his neck. Five men came running across the long grass from a collection of cars and a mechanical digger parked nearby, barely visible in the late afternoon twilight.

"Well done Ben," said one man climbing down the ladder and obviously in charge of everything, "Bring some more lights please, it'll be dark soon. Let's see, what have we got here?"

"I think it's him Dr. Salter," panted Ben, "only this is just the corner. We've been digging in slightly the wrong place. We'll have to widen the hole to uncover the rest of it."

Dr. Salter, a man half Ben's age, looked up at the others standing on the rim of the hole, each now with a lantern in his hand, "What do you think? It's half past four. Shall we come back tomorrow or work a bit longer? It's up to you."

They glanced at each other, "We'll all stay." said one of them.

"Good. Bring the JCB over and widen the hole about three metres that way. We'll need the spotlights on first. You can go if you want Ben. You've done more than your share of the digging today. You must be exhausted."

"I'm probably fitter than you, Dr. Salter, and it's not every day I get to dig up a real live highwayman- I mean a dead one! No I'll stay. Don't forget I'm a volunteer so this is my own unpaid fun time."

Dr. Salter laughed and knelt down to examine the coffin lid - poking it with a small trowel. "It's in good condition considering it's two hundred years old," then almost sang the words, "This is getting ex-cit-ing." He stood up. "That's the JCB starting up. We'd better get out. No, after you. I'll hold the ladder. Do you fancy some tea? I've a flask in the Land Rover."

Minutes later they sat in the warm, comfortable cab peering through the windscreen at the men working with the digger - the whole scene lit by the stark glare of the spotlights. "It's like some sort of historical pageant," said Ben.

"Well it is a sort of drama, when you think about it, thanks to your discovery. More dramatic than the crime itself which was pretty sordid and the execution was miserable and disgusting as always, with half the local population watching. Do you want more tea? Biscuits? Chocolate? You're the hero. Have anything you want."

"No thanks. Listen. This man, Robert Snook, all I know about him is that he was a highwayman who robbed a post boy and he was hung just here where he did it - is that right? Probably Hemel Hempstead's only claim to fame, apart from the Buncefield Oil Depot explosion. You could tell me more about him if we have time."

"OK. It won't take long because we only know a few actual facts. His real name was James Snook but Robert probably comes from him being called robber Snook."

"How did they catch him?"

"Please. I've told this story so many times it will be easier for me if I start at the beginning with the crime itself. This happened one Sunday evening, here on Box Moor in May 1801. He robbed a post boy called John Stevens who was carrying papers and money from Tring to Hemel Hempstead. The Postmaster General put up a reward of two hundred pounds for his arrest. What's that in modern money? More than twenty thousand at least. Ironically he was captured by some other post boys in Marlborough Forest, one of whom spotted him because he knew him from earlier years in Hungerford where he and Snook grew up. The robbery victim, John Stevens, said he couldn't identify him because it was dark at the time but the crucial piece of evidence was a huge bank note that Snook tried to spend in London. The usual punishment for highway robbery was deportation but it was decided to make an example of him so he was sentenced to hang at the scene of his crime. He was held overnight at The Swan public house which you can see over there through the trees. From there he is supposed to have called to the crowd going to the scene of the execution, "No need to hurry, they won't start without me," or something similar. He was buried near the gallows without a coffin but apparently the next day some local people donated one. His body was dug up and then reburied in it the next day."

"And why are we digging him up again now?"

"Because of a proposed new slip road to the A41 by-pass. I don't think it'll ever be built but they offered me a six month window to do some excavation - so here we are."

Half an hour later, Dr. Salter climbed down the ladder and found himself looking at the now completely exposed coffin. There were no marks or writing on the lid.

"Okay. Can you come down and have a go at lifting it out now please gentlemen?"

Six spades were eased down between the sides of the coffin and the wet clay.

"After three. One…two..three."   Six pairs of hands pressed down on the spade handles and accompanied by grunts from the men and by loud squelching from the soggy clay the coffin was levered up enough for two planks to be placed underneath. Four men climbed out of the grave leaving Dr. Salter and Ben to attach four ropes to the planks. Dr. Salter stood up shading his eyes against the powerful lights above, his breath clearly visible in the glare. "Thank you gentlemen… if you're ready… try and pull together and keep it level. I'll tell you if it tilts too much."

The two men stood back against the side of the hole to watch the coffin's receding silhouette ascending to the circle of eager faces above. They scrambled up the ladder as the precious load reached the top and was laid on the ground. "It doesn't weigh much, perhaps it's empty," said one of the men, lifting one end with the toe of his boot.

"Careful!" said Dr. Salter, "It's a bit fragile. If we lift

it by the planks we can carry it into the hut and leave it on the table.It'll be quite secure in there and we can open it in the morning." By now a small crowd of twenty or so people had arrived. They followed in silence at a respectful distance. It could well have been a scene from a Shakespearean tragedy. Several cars stopped on the nearby main road to watch the drama. From there they could see the little procession of tired but happy men trudging through a knee-high carpet of white mist lit by the searchlights and bobbing lanterns. Their progress was also being watched by a disinterested group of Belted Galloway cows with breath steaming from their nostrils.

Inside the hut there was very little standing room around the table. Everyone looked at Dr.Salter. "You want me to open it now don't you?" he smiled, raising his hands like a surgeon. "Very well then…. scalpel… I mean hammer… chisel… lever…" The lid was soon freed from its crumbling and rusted nails. Heads and shoulders leant forward as far as they could go to the sound of a mass intake of breath. There was indeed a skeleton, smaller than everyone expected but all the bones were more or less in place. The skull had a full set of healthy teeth and grinned a welcome to the doctor and the awe-struck workmen. Tangled around bones of the left hand was a small St. Christopher medallion on a chain. After a short silence Dr. Salter spoke very seriously and quietly, "There is one thing I can tell you straight away. Even though I'm not a medical doctor I know a bit about human anatomy and one thing is pretty certain, there ought to be an inquest or something similar. It's obvious to me by looking at the skeleton that these are not the remains of James Snook. That there is a female pelvic bone. This was a woman and in her twenties by the look of the teeth. So who was she, and what happened to Mr. Snook?"

Chapter Two

House buying

A little less than two months later and two miles from the highwayman's grave, the residents of Hemel Hempstead were enjoying the hottest first day of April that anyone could remember. In one of the estate agent offices that had replaced so many of the stores in the shopping parade, four young men and one young woman sat behind desks facing the sun-lit street. They all wore grey suits with white shirts and identical light blue and black striped ties. The men slouched and talked football and cars. They appeared to have bought their suits in great haste from charity shops. The woman sat with a vertical spine and seemed to have employed an expensive tailor. They all looked up hopefully as the door opened but she was the first to speak "Can I help you ...."

"Yes," interrupted a young man striding up to her desk, "number one Herbert Street."

Moments later a grey filing cabinet slid open and he was handed A4 papers with house details and photographs. "Are you particularly wanting a two bedroom house in the old town area?"

"Yes," he murmured, showing her the palm of his hand

for silence while he read, "I want this one," he said at last, sitting down on a chair by her desk and offering her a seat. "Is there a chain and how long has it been on the market?"

"No chain- because the owners have already bought another property in Scotland."

"Well, I think you're going to like me as a customer. I have cash - I mean, I don't need a mortgage. I know it's been up for sale for a while so it must be over priced so will you please offer them twenty per cent less?"

"Would you like to view the property?"

"No. Well not just yet. I'm not much interested in what it's like but I will buy it as long as the surveyor confirms the value. Please tell the owners I'm serious and can put down a large deposit at any time and can pay as soon as the legal stuff is done."

"I can phone them and make an offer while you're here if you like."

"All right. Now is good. I like 'now'."

She dialled a number - trying not to look too excited, "Hello Mr. Finch, it's Susan from Fensons. We have an offer for your house. ...Yes...." she wound some of her blond hair round her index finger, "The customer doesn't have a property to sell and can pay without a mortgage... That's right. However he is offering twenty per cent less than your asking price, that's £200,000... Yes I know ... but ...would you like to think about it and ring me back? .... Oh..... I'll see what he says," she covered the telephone with her hand, "They say what about ten per cent?"

"Fifteen."

"He says fifteen...........," she looked at him over the top of her glasses, smiling, "Twelve?"

" Twelve? That's £220,000.....Ok. Final offer to be agreed now."

"Right Mr. Finch, £220,000 if you agree now……….
right … thank you, Mr. Finch." She put down the phone.

"Well?"

"They accept your offer. Now can I have your name
and few details? Congratulations by the way, it's a very
sought-after area as they say, especially Herbert Street,
Mr….?

"Street…. Herbert Street."

"Just a minute, is this a wind-up?" her smile disappeared
and her voice became quieter. "I do know what day it is
today."

"No. It's my real name. Honest. Look, here's my
driving licence and my bankcards. I'm a photographer and
I'm moving into the area. I need to get known. My main
reason for buying the house is for the address. I might
not even live there. I'll probably let it out to someone on
condition they forward my mail. People remember things
like strange addresses and names. My full name is John
Herbert Street. Here's my card. No address on it yet, just
my mobile phone number. People who like me call me
John but Herbert Street of Herbert Street, photographer,
will have a certain ring to it, don't you think?"

"I won't forget it for a while anyway." She was smiling
again, "You're not the usual customer we get here."

"You're not the sort of estate agent I'm used to either.
I think I would like to see the property, now I've almost
bought it."

"Would you like me to arrange it?"

"Well, now would be better."

"Now?"

"Yes please – I like 'now', and why not? You must
have the keys because the owners are in Scotland and
you're not exactly rushed off your feet this morning." He

smiled. "One of the others can show me if you like…. If you think I might attack you or something."

"I'd like to see you try. I'd break your neck in two places" she smiled sweetly. Then to her colleagues, who were straining their ears to catch the conversation, she said in a louder voice "I'm just taking a customer to Herbert Street." She rattled her way through four rows of keys on the wall, "Here we are. I can drive you there if you like but it will be quicker to walk - it's very close."

Minutes later they were walking towards the old part of town feeling the sun on their backs. It would have seemed to anyone watching that they were studying their sharp edged shadows that preceded them on the cracked and stained pavement. His shadow was quite a lot longer than hers. The truth was that they were rapidly becoming aware of the attraction they held for each other. This surprised them both so they were avoiding eye contact. They simultaneously felt increasingly vulnerable and, unlike a few minutes before when each couldn't care less what the other thought, they now used softer voices and tried not to offend. Susan spoke first and dared to look at her client directly, "You said that we weren't what you are used to. Why are we so different than other estate agents?"

"I didn't say agents - I said agent. I was talking about you."

"Okay then, how am I different?"

"Well….." He too made eye contact but immediately went back to shadow studying, "Here we go. You listened to me, and believed me, apart from a little blip when I told you my name, and you're very intelligent and smart - unlike your colleagues who look like they need somebody to get them dressed in the morning."

"Is there anything else you think you know about me?"

"You try to minimise your attractiveness but it doesn't work- with the suit I mean, and the glasses which you don't need of course."

"What makes you think I don't need them?"

"I'm a photographer remember. I know about lenses. My great aunt's spectacles were so strong that one sunny day she put them down on a picnic basket and burnt a hole in it. Yours are just flat pieces of glass."

They stopped at a zebra crossing. She was blushing slightly as she glanced at his jeans and boring jumper, "And how do you hide your attractiveness?"

"I'm not hiding anything. I'm not attractive!

No really. I know I'm not handsome. I'm glad of that. Handsome men are usually womanisers or boring celebrities, or gay or something."

"My brother is good looking and gay."

"Oh come on. Am I supposed to feel I've said the wrong thing? I'm sure he's a wonderful man and I would like him a lot especially if he's your brother. He's your older brother."

"How do you know that - or are you just guessing to try to look clever?"

"I am guessing but I'm right aren't I... and you're a second child?"

"I might be. Why?"

"It's just that second children are often very similar in character. They're usually more attention seeking, and often become partners with other second children. It's supposed to be something to do with feeling they don't get as much love and attention as their older siblings."

"Rubbish! What are you a sociologist as well as a photographer?" They had been walking quickly and talking so much they paused to catch their breath just before Herbert Street. "Oh I get it. Now you're going to say you're a second child."

"Yes of course I am," and then with mock coyness with his hand on his heart, "but I wouldn't presume….."

"No don't," she said, but smiled as they walked on, shadow studying again.

"Okay, look. How many couples do you know who are second children?"

She paused, looked up at the sky and then made eye contact again, "All right, yes. My parents, my uncle and aunt, my best friend and her husband .... no, actually three of my friends and their partners…. but listen, I told you, I'm different. Now, stimulating as this conversation is, can we leave it now? We're here; end-of- terrace, two bedroom Victorian house in the much sort-after Old Town area……Welcome to number one, Herbert Street, Mr. Street."

"Oh call me John, please, Susan."

"Mr. Street is better, it's more professional to be formal."

"Okay then, what's your surname?"

"Savage. I'm Susan Savage."

"Miss?"

"Ms."

"Nice to meet you Ms Savage," he held out his hand.

"And you, Mr. Street." She ignored his hand and opened the door. They stepped into a dark hallway, both enjoying the coolness after the heat outside, she going ahead and opening doors, he absorbing everything very intensely, turning on taps and looking in cupboards. She walked through the kitchen and opened the back door to the garden. "It's very clean," he shouted down the stairs to her, "Won't need a lot of decorating and it's furnished and everything. Nice bedrooms and one of the beds is huge. It must be extra king size. I'll need that with my long arms and legs. It's just like they are still living here …where are you?"

"I'm in the garden, such as it is." He found her sitting halfway down the weathered steep brick steps that led down to the garden. She had taken off her jacket and was basking in the sunshine holding her knees and staring at a moss-covered birdbath at the bottom of the steps. He stopped in the doorway as she turned to look at him, her straight blond hair catching the sun. He said nothing.

"What?" she asked, "Oh yes, Mister photographer, you're going to say how beautiful my blond hair is in the sunlight?" Laughing, she lifted her glasses for a moment, "Do you want to see my fantastic blue eyes as well?"

"You've got a funny way of selling a house."

"You've got a funny way of buying one. Do you still want it?" she asked, getting up.

"Oh yes. I might even live in it."

"Really. That's nice. I'd like that." She walked down to the tiny garden.

"And why would you like me living here?" he asked, following her. She strode past him, filled a watering can at a tap by the house, came back and began to top up the birdbath. He stood close to her. She didn't seem to mind and looked right into his face, "I ought to tell you something. This is my place. I'm selling it to you."

"Well then, who the hell is Mr. Finch in Scotland?"

"I'm sorry," she looked away, "He doesn't exist. It was stupid of me. To be honest you threw me for a bit. I don't know what I was thinking because I would have had to tell you eventually. Somehow it was easier for me to negotiate a price without you knowing I was the owner.

Do you forgive me?" She held out her hand. He looked at her suspiciously for a moment then kissed the back of her hand in mock gallantry. She willingly let him keep holding it as she climbed the steps and looked down at him in queenly manner.

"And why is her majesty selling her palace?"

"I'm buying somewhere else."

"A bigger house?"

"No. You can let go of my hand now. Look, I'm not trying to be mysterious, it's just a bit complicated that's all. There will be a lot of work to do on my new property before I can live in it so I shall have to rent somewhere while the work is going on. Don't worry there won't be any problems as far as you're concerned. You can buy this place as soon as you like - or not - it doesn't matter to me. The person I'm buying from is going to retire to Spain. He just wants the money for spending but he's in no hurry."

"Do you live here then?"

"Sometimes. I travel a lot. I have another job as well as this one. It involves moving around quite a bit. No. I'm not going to tell you what it is so don't ask." She went into the kitchen and hung her jacket on a peg on the inside of the door, "Do you want a coffee?"

"Yes please. Milk, no sugar."

They stood facing each other leaning against the black marble worktops fitted to both sides of the little kitchen. Susan held her mug close to her face to smell the coffee. The mug had a photograph of a meerkat on it. The handle had long since broken off and to save hurting her fingers she held it in a tea towel with 'Welcome to Hemel Hempstead' printed on it. "What?" she asked, "I like meerkats.... Is that all right? And I've had this mug for years. I always seem to have happy times with...." She blushed. John wondered if her large pupils were the result of moving into the dimly lit kitchen after the sunlight outside. "You do seem very much at home here," he said softly. It was very quiet indoors and they were both silent as they each wondered what the other was thinking. Then thoughts welled up inside them and both tried to speak at the same time, Susan ahead by a microsecond.

"I wonder if you would consider……"

"What do think of this idea…….. no no. You first," said John.

"Well… what do you think about me being your tenant?"

"OK. You said you were going to have to find somewhere to rent so I was just going to suggest it."

"So, you listen to people too - and you did say I was going to like you as a customer."

"Just as a customer?"

"Let's keep this professional, how much will you want a month?"

"Dunno. No seriously - whatever the going rate is. Slightly less if you like because it would save me money advertising for someone – and paying ten per cent to one of you rip off agents!"

"Okay. Done!"

"Do you smoke."

"No. Do you?"

"No. I shall need to see your references!"

"Of course."

"Only kidding."

"I know."

Silence for a moment.

John spoke quickly, "Listen. This house has one bathroom but each bedroom has it's own loo and a shower - I mean would you consider being my lodger instead of renting the whole house? You could live here almost without me ever seeing or talking to you - and I fully understand you could break my neck in two places if I did. Seriously, the rent would be a lot less for you so you could spend more on your new build - and I wouldn't have to find somewhere else...." They stood looking directly at each other for a short while without any embarrassment.

Susan slowly placed her coffee mug in the sink. "It seems we might have a very satisfactory arrangement. Have you finished your coffee?" He hurriedly turned to pick up his mug and knocked it off the worktop. She caught it in mid-air but in doing so splashed the remains of the coffee on his jeans.

"Sorry," he said, "I'm not usually clumsy, honest."

"I know. It's the stress," she laughed as she attempted to wipe his jeans with the kitchen towel.

"I'll do that." He grabbed the towel too and they had a mock tug of war with it. They stopped pulling and looked at each other – neither of them letting go. "Which bedroom will you want Ms Savage," he asked quietly.

"Lets go and decide shall we, Mr. Street." They climbed the stairs, Susan first, pulling John by means of the tea towel. They dropped it as Susan's mobile phone rang. She sat on a step to answer it, taking off her shoes as John disappeared upstairs. "Hello Michael. Yes. We've finished here but we're going have lunch and look at some other places... ...no, just at the exteriors to compare properties but I think he's settled for Herbert Street.... Yes, that's his name, bizarre isn't it? ...... I won't be back this afternoon. See you first thing tomorrow.... Cheers." She switched off her phone, threw it onto the tea towel next to her shoes and began to climb the stairs. She stopped for a moment and added her glasses to the pile.

Back at her office Michael slowly put down the phone as he stared out of the window. One of his colleagues asked him, "Was that Susan? I thought she was keen on lunching with us at the new pub up the road."

Michael tilted his chair back, put his hands in his pockets and put his feet on the desk, "So did I." He exchanged glances with his colleague. Then he added, very quietly, "The lucky bastard."

Chapter Three

Ben Carter's Place

The bright April sunshine was also warming Ben Carter as he sat on the veranda of his residence in the woods to the north of the town. The veranda (he called it his cowboy porch) was purpose built on the south side of his house making an ideal place to sit in his rocking chair and think. He was thinking about the woman whose remains he had dug up two months earlier.

His house was different, unusual, a shack really. No one knew exactly how long he had been living there because his home had always been hidden from view amongst the trees. The land, four acres of woodland with the River Gade running through it, belonged to him. The original building was an old RAF hut used as a stable for two horses but over the years he had built a lot of extra living space, workshops and even an artist's studio. A surveyor, should one ever set foot in the place, would have difficulty deciding what each room was used for as they all contained products of his inventive brains. The kitchen table was often littered with plumbing bits, spanners and timber while some of the workshops had kettles, refrigerators and were well equipped for working lunches. Two 1970's caravans had been attached to the stable to make extra rooms. This was achieved by the simple method of lining up the door of the caravan with a suitable aperture in the main building and nailing the two together. One of these annexes was his bedroom, the other he described as the "guest room" which had only been used by members of his family on rare occasions. This was not because it was in any way unsavoury or ill equipped. On the contrary, it was warm and clean with an en-suite toilet and shower, a double bed and two bunks in it - unlike his own annex room which had one bed, and a wardrobe containing an expensive but ancient suit and four shirts. There were piles of clothes on the floor but if there was anyone there to listen he would tell them that they were clean clothes and that he knew where everything was - which was absolutely true.

The reason there was often no one to listen to him was because he lived alone having separated from his wife fifteen years earlier. They had four children who had been living with his wife until recently but now she was alone because they had all grown up, left home and married. Each of their children had provided their parents with a grandchild. During the fairly amicable separation the family home was sold and Ben bought the four acres of woodland without any real intention of living there. As he put it, "It just sort of happened." For a while he lived in rented accommodation in the town but found himself spending more and more time on his patch of land. He made some improvements to the old hut in the form of insulation and a wood-burning stove. Then he saw an advertisement in the local Gazette for four double glazed windows and a set of patio doors for £100, "buyer collects." So he bought and collected them and discovered they were different sizes, colours and design but happily fitted them to his hut in one afternoon with the help of his son who told him he was mad.

"I know son, I know," he sighed, "but I'm saner than most." He stood back and looked at his building with great fondness and then went inside, deep in thought. He opened one of the windows to speak to his son again. "David," he said quietly, "You'll think I'm even more crazy now, and I don't want you to tell anyone yet, but I've just decided I'm going to live here."

"Dad, no!"

"Now don't get all disapproving. I've made up my mind. Perhaps it'll change your view if I tell you I can stop paying rent at £800 a month - so you kids can have two hundred of that each….. There, I thought that might shut you up."

This was about the time when he decided to retire from his job as a press photographer. He had earned a lot and spent a lot during his thirty years working for a national newspaper, 'snappin' as he called it. He had been prudent enough to invest in a substantial private pension which, ten years ago at the age of 50, provided him with enough to live on and still be able to contribute towards the upkeep of his ex-wife and his children. His dream was to be a portrait painter, hence the studio attached to his strange residence. It was a beautiful room with a north-facing skylight and two enormous plate-glass windows which once adorned the front of a car showroom in the old town. He wasn't very successful. This was not because he wasn't a good painter; on the contrary his portraits were excellent and delighted everyone including the sitters and their friends and relatives. The problem was with the artist. He was inclined to ask people if he could paint them and eventually he would give them his finished work for nothing. Refusing commissions from well off patrons just because he disliked them was not good business but he seemed unable, or more likely unwilling, to do anything about it. "You just swan about," his ex wife would say with great bitterness, "painting beautiful women..."

"They're not all beautiful women. I paint old men and women and children as well."

"Mostly beautiful and young women and then you give the pictures away!"

"That's true."

"Why can't you take a commission now and again? Make some real money."

However his tactics were not entirely without purpose - by now there were a great many portraits on the walls of houses in Hemel Hempstead and in quite a few other homes in England and around the world. He was building up quite a reputation and people wanting to commission him were offering more and more money.

"Eventually," he told his wife, "people I actually want to paint will pay me good money."

He made many machines. Not all of them original inventions but all of them used and useful. He secretly diverted part of the river to a dam with a water wheel which provided him with a small amount of electricity which he supplemented with a petrol generator when he needed more. The sloping roofs of four hen houses were actually home-made solar panels which supplied him with plenty of free hot water from March to October. On winter days and nights he kept warm with his beloved wood-burning stove which also gave him hot water for washing as well as heating six old iron radiators he had acquired from scrap merchants. However his most glorious machine was his treadmill. This was made from an old wooden brewer's fermenting vessel four metres in diameter and ten metres long. It could contain up to eight people running or walking side by side and electricity was produced by means of two alternators, one on each end of the drum and connected to a bank of lorry batteries to store the power. It also provided enough energy to power a television which hung from wires at a suitable height for those working the treadmill. Ben wouldn't allow a television in his house and his idea was to discourage his grandchildren from watching rubbish programs. However they thought it was wonderful fun and would work the treadmill for hours whilst watching the most appalling programs. He also loaned it to local fitness and running clubs. He claimed in advertisements that it was "a wonderful way to lose weight and get fit - and absolutely free."

He did think of charging people for using it but thought that it would be a bit unfair.

Between painting and making machines he managed to find time for volunteering for local historical and archaeological societies where he recently became famous as the "man who dug up the mystery woman." Now, like many other people in the town, he often found himself trying to think of a rational explanation for her being in the grave. "Maybe his sister or cousin took his place," he thought to himself, "no ...there were so many people who knew Snook and witnessed his trial and execution.... no...daft idea. That's the stuff of kid's adventure stories. Perhaps she was actually a highway woman, and was a bit butch-looking and had a deep voice."

"I don't suppose we will ever know," Ben said out loud. He stood up, yawned, and stretched his arms hitting the oil-lamp hanging directly above his head. "Damn! I'm always bloody doing that," he muttered, rubbing his knuckles, "I wonder what the time is. Where's me phone.? Nearly five o'clock. Susan was going to call me this afternoon. Dozy cow..........Hello Susan …. you okay? You sound a bit sleepy. No, don't apologise...I'd almost forgotten as well. It must be the warm weather. Like I said I'm in no hurry but do you still want to buy this place?......"

Chapter Four

Everything is now

"Yes Ben, most definitely I want to buy it." Susan sat on the stairs with the telephone and wearing her lover's jumper as a dressing gown. The sleeves were so long on her they hung off her arms like elephant trunks. John was crossing the landing on the way to the bathroom and noticed Susan crouching below. Her voice was the only evidence of who she was because her head was down by her knees and the rest of her was hidden under a flood of blond hair and the jumper. To give the impression that he had no interest in what she was doing he went for his shower singing, "Swing low sweet char-i-ot" in his best bass voice.

"And it seems I can pay you very soon as I now have a buyer for my place......... Yes, this afternoon... and he hasn't got a property to sell. He's paying for it in cash... No not literally. I mean he doesn't have a mortgage. So there we are. I'll be able to give you a deposit soon if he does the same for me. Talk to you soon. Bye." She climbed the stairs and listened happily to John singing as she waited to ambush him coming out of the bathroom.

"coming for to.... carry.. .me... home! YIPES !!" As he

opened the door Susan leapt up and clung to him with her arms and legs, biting his ear and covering him in kisses. "I say. Steady on old girl!" he exclaimed in a mock cavalry officer voice, "I thought we'd done all that affection nonsense – and I'm all wet."

"I know, and clean and fresh and your hair smells nice and I want to eat you."

"Well you can't right now," he said, gently but firmly lowering her to the ground. "Seriously, I have to get dressed and go."

"Where?"

"I have to meet the Gazette editor at half past six in The Old Bell pub. Very informal but I don't want to be late. He said he might be able to give me some work. They don't have enough photographers to cover, apparently. Also I was thinking of suggesting the paper did a story about me and the Herbert Street name thing. What do you think?"

Susan looked disappointed with having to deal with reality. "Fine, I suppose, but please don't mention me. It's to do with my other job. I need to keep a low profile, for a while anyway. Don't look at me like that. I'll tell you all about it one day soon."

"You MI5 spies are all the same."

"No. It's nothing like that," She followed him into the bedroom and John began dressing, "it's just part of my contract not to tell anyone what I do. I'll give you the number of my estate agent boss if you want a quote about the house for the paper. He doesn't know about my other job so don't ask him."

"I won't," said John, hopping round in a circle while he pulled his socks on.   Susan, still wearing John's jumper, was spinning the dangling ends of the sleeves and looking like a twin propeller aeroplane. She was looking pensive, "Can I ask you something? Will it make you late?"

"Depends if you want the meaning of life. What's the time?"

"Half past five."

"Fire away then. I'll have to go in twenty minutes."

Susan paced up and down the room still spinning her propellers, "I suppose this is a mini cliché- you know - 'where are we going with this?' me ..you..us sort of thing. I don't need to have our futures mapped out in detail.... Actually that would be rather nice I think, but quite impractical, no... you know what I'm asking, I can see it in your face."

"Yes I do."

Susan was now speaking very quickly. "OK tell me - what you feel-what you want. Myself, I'm infatuated. I can only just keep my hands off you. I rather like being ecstatic but it's making me feel a bit anxious. I'm a confirmed pessimist - it's a safety net thing- the only way I can deal with extreme happiness - so I've told myself it won't last - but I want it to.I could pretend to be all cool and aloof -but that wouldn't be true - like Mr. Finch in Scotland wasn't true. I want honesty. OK, I'm calm now. Can we start with 'When will I see you next?' That would be nice."

John stepped into her flight-path, grabbed hold of her propellers and looked straight into her eyes,

"Right, listen."

"I'm listening - all cool and aloof. Aloof is a funny word - sounds like something you scrub your back with....."

"Please shut up."

"Right."

"Sit."

"OK"

They sat down together on the side of the extra king sized bed. This time it was John who seemed to have difficulty speaking his mind but after a short pause he spoke slowly and deliberately, swallowing now and again as if his throat was a little dry, "This is going to be a bit of a speech too, but first things first. Yes I would like to see you very soon. In fact I was going to ask if you would like some dinner in The Old Bell when I've finished with the editor. Would about half past seven be all right?" Susan nodded vigorously. "Good. First of all thank you for being brave enough to speak like that. I say 'brave' because I think I should have spoken first. You're ahead of me. I thought I was supposed to be the "now" person. OK next. Be assured, be very assured. I'm here for the long term if you want me. As to how I feel - I'm really, really happy. Like you I'm a bit scared but this is too good to feel apprehensive about. Monet used to say painting a picture was like jumping into the water and then seeing if you can swim. That's what it's like for us I think. We seem to be pretty good swimmers and the water is wonderful so this is fantastic. This is now. You know why I like that word? Everything is now. All that there is is now. You can remember things and hope for things in the future but all you are doing is stretching a bit of 'now' - a few hours or days either way. All I can say is you're the best 'now' that's ever happened to me. I've never done this before -well no, what I mean is I've never met anyone that I've been like this with, especially in such an amazingly short time. I'm not going to say the 'L' word just yet because to be honest I never know what it means - when I do I shall say it often - when we are old probably. Is that all right?"

"Perfectly."

"I really would like to kiss you now."

"But I hardly know you!"

"That's true!" They came together, slowly, carefully, delicately, like docking space vehicles.

"Haven't we done this yet?"

"Not like this we haven't."

A few seconds passed in Hemel Hempstead while they travelled to the end of the universe and back.

Susan flung herself backwards on to the bed, "Lemons!" she said loudly.

"What?"

"Kissing, touching, having sex, it's so sweet it hurts - like sucking lemons. Don't you think?"

"You're raving mad. Can I have my jumper back now please? Thank you. I've got to go. Good-bye. See you at seven thirty."

Susan got up, wrapped a sheet around herself and went to the window to watch him walking down Herbert Street towards The Old Bell. She turned round smiling gleefully with one of her fingers in her mouth.. Her eyes moved from side to side as she viewed her now completely wrecked bedroom. "Wheeee!" she shouted as she ran across the room and got her legs tangled up in the sheet. She tripped, performed an involuntary forward roll across the bed and finished head down in the gap between the bed and the wall with her feet kicking wildly in the air.

Chapter Five

Green Ink

Meanwhile, back at the strange house in the woods, Ben left his rocking chair on the veranda and ambled down to the edge of the river. He stared into the water and thought of the Mayor of Hemel Hempstead, Councillor Mrs. Daphne Mallacott. He hated her. She was the one, when she was a fairly new councillor with the planning committee, who had discovered his secret dwelling and was the main instigator in trying to get him and all his constructions removed from the property. This, he conceded, she had every right to do and he always knew he might be discovered one day BUT, and it was a very big 'but', it was the way she went about it which gave birth to his simmering rage. She arrived smiling on his doorstep one morning, presumably after some kind of tip-off, overweight with a lifeboat chin, lipstick on her teeth and smelling of some kind of cheap scent. Ben loathed women who smelt of cheap scent and had lipstick on their teeth.

"Am I speaking to the owner of this property?"

"You are," said Ben.

"Then you must be Benjamin Carter according to the land register." She held up an A4 photocopy.

"I am," said Ben.

She offered her gloved hand but Ben ignored it "I am Councillor Mallacott. I am on the planning committee and I have been told that you are living here permanently and there is no planning permission for a dwelling." Ben said nothing but looked directly into her face. "I'll take that as a 'yes' shall I?"

There was a pause before Ben answered slowly, "Officially I live at 202, Marlins Turn. That's where my wife lives but we are separated. My mail is still delivered there but it is true that I have been staying here for a while."

"Well you can't, not without planning consent."

Ben watched as she wrote down his address with a fountain pen with green ink. Ben also hated people who wrote things in green ink. His piano teacher used green ink to complain to his parents that he had not practised enough. "All right. What happens now?"

"Putting it simply you will have to leave the site and this building will have to be taken down. It is an eyesore. These contraptions will have to go as well."

"Part of the building was here years before I bought the land and how can it be an eyesore when no one can see it?"

"You will have to take that up with the planning encouragement officer who will be visiting the site very shortly I expect."

"Don't you mean enforcement officer."

"That's what I said."

"Any idea when that will be?"

"I expect you will be sent a letter to your address, 202, Marlins Turn, I think you said." Smiling with satisfaction she turned to go. "You look a little sad Mr. Carter. Of course you are free to make a reflective planning application."

"Oh you mean a retrospective application."

"Yes exactly. Didn't you hear what I said? You might be able to show a plausible reason for living here. We're not robots on the council you know. Don't forget I am on the committee and will take everyone's interests into consideration - including yours. Make an application Mr. Carter. I will look out for it." *'I bet you will, you cow,'* thought Ben. She offered her hand again and this time Ben shook it despite the glove. Her smile became even wider showing even more lipstick teeth. "Good luck Mr. Carter. I wish you well."

'*Like hell you do,'* thought Ben but said, "And you too, Councillor, Good bye."

A week later Ben met the enforcement officer and they sat on the veranda having much the same conversation as with the councillor. As before he was encouraged to put in an application. "Three hundred and fifty quid?," exclaimed Ben, "That's a bit steep isn't it?" But he went ahead, paid his money, made six copies of the forms and maps and handed everything in to the town hall. The day after his cheque was cashed he was sent an enforcement order to stop living in the property and an accompanying letter advising him that planning consent was likely to be refused. '"Why the hell did they take my money then?" he asked himself. He telephoned the planning office who refused to give him his money back as his 'application was already being processed'.He left many messages on Councillor Mallacott's answer phone but never received a reply. Ben resigned himself to his fate until he received a letter from the council saying that his case was going before the planning committee. This seemed to spur the councillor into all sorts of strange activities. After ignoring Ben completely she now sent him letters accusing him of all sorts of misbehaviour and nuisance which he happily decided not to reply to. He heard from various sources that she was becoming obsessed with his case. At one stage he spotted her lurking in the trees taking photographs of the building. He moved some buckets to make a noise, but behaved as if he was unaware of her presence. Minutes later he spotted her walking away with her head down trying to hide behind the bushes on the way to her car.

He decided to consult a solicitor. He tried several in the town without much success until one of them, a young man who looked like Count Dracula and never smiled, interrogated him for five minutes as if he was in the dock and then said he would take the case. "It will cost you between fifteen hundred and three thousand pounds but I'm almost certain we will win."

"How much? !!!!"

"Oh. Don't worry about the cost. Just think how much more the property will be worth if we succeed."

"It's all right for you to say that. You won't lose out if it goes wrong. You people never do."

"I think you might be surprised by how often "we people" take risks, Mr. Carter. I can tell you I don't take on cases if I don't think I can win." He leant on his elbows and pressed his fingertips together.

'I thought solicitors only did that in films,' thought Ben.

"If you can prove you have been living there for more than ten years without being challenged, or causing nuisance or being noticed even, then you don't need planning permission. We will apply for what is called a Certificate of Lawfulness. Can't see any problem. I will want fifteen hundred pounds in advance. Thank you and good bye Mr. Carter."

And so it was. Ben won his case. Councillor Mallacott was consumed with rage. She dedicated her life to ruining Ben's progress by any means she could. She made sure that the building was immediately condemned as being unsafe and not conforming to building regulations. This was heart breaking for him , and, having very little money left after paying the solicitor, there was no way he could afford to build a decent house so he decided to sell. The first estate agent he spoke to happened to be Susan Savage who offered to buy his property for herself.

The hatred he had for his nemesis councillor grew and grew. He couldn't forget how vicious she had been to him especially after his victory. It was her hypocrisy too. He had heard from various people how devious she had been with developing her own house and flouting planning law with other properties she owned. "What a nasty bit of work," he said to himself. "How she ever came to be mayor I shall never know."

He was sorry to have to give up his land but had no regrets about going to live in Spain. "I've had enough of this crappy town. Who wants to live in a place that would have types like her on the council and even have her as mayor? I would really like to see her get her comeuppance. She and all her lousy friends can go to hell for all I care."

Chapter Six

Self Defence

At one of the tables in the long room which was the dining area of The Old Bell John sat on his own writing in a notebook. Under the notebook was an open leather folder containing a stack of photographs and press cuttings. There were half a dozen diners nearby and a few drinkers sitting at the dimly lit bar some distance away from the tables.

"Is this seat taken?" Susan stood before him in a pair of blue jeans and a white T-shirt. She had washed her hair and now wore it tied back in a ponytail with a few strands hanging down her cheeks and tucked behind her ears.

John stood up and pulled a chair out for her. "Well I was waiting for someone - bit like you only all smartly dressed and unapproachable and wearing glasses."

Susan smiled, "I thought I would wear something as un-suit-like as possible."

"I think you look fantastic."

"Well get used to it. This is me. This is the sort of thing I wear all the time when I'm not estate-agenting and you did say your meeting was informal. How did it go?"

"Oh fine. You've just missed him. Nice bloke. Young.

Just a bit older than me I would say - twenty eight, maybe thirty. I'm twenty seven by the way."

"I'm twenty five. When's your birthday?"

"June the twentieth. Yours?"

"February the fourth."

"That's a daft day for a birthday. Nobody ever gets born in February. How do you celebrate it? With mine I usually have a garden party or a river trip in the glorious sunshine."

"Well get you!"

"Don't worry. I'll take you to the Caribbean or India or somewhere."

"Make sure you do. Anyway what happened?"

"He wants me to work for him! Starting tomorrow, Friday. It is Thursday today isn't it? I'm losing track of time with all that's happening to me at the minute. It's your fault. You've done something to my mind. Anyway Friday, all day Saturday and most of the evening. Freelance work to start with. The pay isn't much but it's better than nothing and it will help to get me known in the area. I told him about the name thing and he's happy to use a picture of me by the Herbert Street sign with a small caption story - when I've bought the house of course."

"So when will I see you?"

"I was thinking of moving my stuff in on Sunday if that's all right-if you'll let me. It's still your house even though we've shaken hands on it."

"I've never heard it called that before."

"If you give me your bank details I will put ten thousand in it tomorrow morning, then you can give it to the owner of the property you are buying - or whatever you like.

"Thank you. You must have heard me talking to him."

"Only that bit. I was trying not to, with the singing and all, but you are quite loud on the phone."

A waitress appeared. Susan picked up one of the menus "Can we eat now? I'm really hungry."

"So am I. I want the salmon salad what about you?"

"I'll have the same and apple pie and ice cream to follow."

"Two salmon salads with apple pies and ice cream please." When they were alone again John leant forward and spoke very quietly, "I have to warn you about something quite serious." he glanced left and right melodramatically, "I am not good at going out to dinner."

"What do you mean. Do you have food fights or throw your potatoes at the wall?"

"No, nothing like that. I get angry. Unreasonably so probably, but it doesn't seem unreasonable to me."

"Thanks for the warning. Does this always happen?"

"Only if I have to wait a long time for the food."

"How does this manifest itself? Do you become threatening and violent?"

"Not so far. I usually walk out of the restaurant without paying - which seems perfectly reasonable to me if they haven't fed you."

"What sort of a delay are we talking about? Five minutes? Half an hour?"

"No. I told you I'm not unreasonable. After three quarters of an hour I get huffy and if it gets to an hour I walk out. Always. Without question."

"I see."

"All right. I'll try and make my case. I go to a restaurant to eat and pay good money to people for the privilege. Simple. I do this because I'm hungry and I want the restaurant to understand this. I don't see any pleasure

35

or any point in sitting at a table getting hungrier and hungrier. If I wanted to do that I could just stay at home, cook myself some dinner and stare at the wall for nearly an hour."

"Don't worry," Susan leant forward and grasped his arm with mock sincerity, "We'll find a way to get through this."

"What's even worse is when you are invited to someone's house for dinner. Then you're really at their mercy. 'Come round about seven and we'll eat at half past', they say. So you have a light lunch, or go without, to give yourself a good appetite, for their sakes as well as yours, and you get there at ten past seven. Then, horror of horrors, she, or even worse, he, is only just putting something into the oven and the veg is sitting in stone cold water in the saucepans. Some of my best friends have done this to me. 'Would you like a drink?' they ask. 'Not really,' I'm thinking, 'I'm bloody hungry and I want to eat something.' When it gets to nine-o'clock and there's still nothing to eat and I've run out of conversation, I become full of suppressed belligerence. I'm convinced my once loved friends are sadists and by now I am so uncomfortable I don't want to eat any of their wonderful food they have been tiddling around with for an eternity. All I want to do is grab a handful of bread, shove it in my mouth and go home, but I can't. I have to be terribly polite and make convincing compliments about stuff which by now I can only just manage to force between my teeth........"

"There. There. You'll just have to join G A, Gorger's Anonymous. You know, sit round in a circle with eight other lost souls, 'I am Herbert Street and I gorge my food. It's been two whole weeks since I walked out of a restaurant without eating'...."

"It isn't gorging. I'm not a glutton either. I can go without food for quite long periods if I need to. The nasty bit is when people thoughtlessly or deliberately make you hungry, promise you food and don't give you any. If these same people did it to a dog they would be guilty of cruelty...."

The smiling waitress appeared with two plates generously loaded with salmon, new potatoes and delicious looking salad. She slipped away blissfully unaware how merciful she and the chef had been.

Susan looked at her watch, "That was twelve minutes."

"Perfect! I told you I wasn't unreasonable."

An hour later they had finished their excellent food and after John had paid the bill with cash and left a generous tip they sat back in their chairs to finish their coffee.

"Your turn to tell me some things you don't like," demanded John."

"Oh, all the usual things. The main ones are misery and boredom - which are much the same I suppose. I know there are much worse things like wars and torture and illness and stuff but these things are really extreme and hopefully don't affect us in everyday life. Misery though - that's awful. People who make other people miserable I really can't forgive. I know I should because they probably have proper excuses but I can't, or more truthfully I won't."

"Tell you what, I'll try my best not to make you miserable if you promise not to cook me food and keep it from me."

"OK, Done."

"Tell me the things you do like."

"That's easy. Meerkats."

"I'm being serious."

"So am I. All right. ....Being in good company-especially when people are laughing. Being on my own but not for long. Not being ill. Being warm in winter and cool in summer. Being abroad as long as the travelling isn't hell. Actually I'm not one for going out to dinner either. I like it now because I'm with you and the food is good but the act of eating doesn't excite me very much. The idea of dining in the best restaurant in the world but on my own fills me with horror. Good food is nice like a good house or a car that doesn't break down - something you need so it pleases you to have it - like money. Discovering new things makes me really happy, like meerkats, or you, or realising that I can do something that I didn't think I would be able to do - like the first time I got up courage to speak to a big audience and best of all realising they actually liked it."

"I go along with all of that, even the meerkats but emotionally, and most of all visually, and even more than you do perhaps, I think that laughing with happiness is the most wonderful thing in the world. I love it on television when they show the audience watching a brilliant comedian. I wish they would have women in the fashion magazines laughing for a change rather than the so-called gorgeous pouting miseries."

"Have you done much fashion photography?"

"Quite a bit but not for the big glossy magazines. That is a whole different world to the one I live in. You have a team working to make the pictures - all terribly clever people - and I wouldn't mind doing it for the money - but really I like making my own ideas succeed and getting the model to work to those ideas. There's more satisfaction that way. Once, working for an evening paper, I was sent to photograph a really experienced fashion model. The story was about her rather than clothes. Anyway I arrive at her fabulous home. She's nice enough to look at, fantastic figure and all that, but then she says, 'Will this dress do?' I say that it'll be fine. 'Good,' she says, and drapes herself over a chair, 'Ready?' I start taking photographs and each time I click she does another pose and after about eight different shots she says, 'That should do it. Have you got enough?' Before I could answer she says, 'Good. You'll have to excuse me I've got to get ready to go out. Bye-ee,' and disappears. I get back to the office and everybody liked the photographs but I felt really strange. I felt I hadn't done anything at all. She might as well have taken the pictures herself with a remote control. Very weird......"

"Can I have a look at your pictures."

"Sure," said John handing her the folder, "Its a dead easy way to sell yourself for a job. You just show your photographs and immediately people know if you are any good or not- especially if you have press cuttings with by-lines. Much better than a CV. What do you think?"

"I think they're good, but then they would be wouldn't they? I like the one with the crow having a fag! Is that real? You didn't fiddle with the image?"

"No. Not at all I swear. It was taken when I was quite young. The crow used to visit my dad on his allotment and one day he gave him one of his lighted cigarettes for a laugh and it took it and held it in it's beak till it had burned down to the ...."

Susan interrupted him, "I think we are going to have company very soon," she whispered, "Don't look now but behind you there are four drunks by the bar who have been looking at me for about fifteen minutes."

"Oh great."

"I'm just preparing you but I think we should ignore them. Any kind of reaction will encourage them. What do you think?"

"Oh I agree totally. I don't want any confrontation either. We'll leave if you like."

"All right, but in a minute. I want to finish my coffee............ Oh here we go."

"Hello luv. You enjoying yourself?" The voice came from a six foot heavily built man with a bulging stomach hanging over his belt. His eyelids were half closed and his speech was slurred. He swayed slightly from side to side and used the back of his hand to catch some uncontrolled saliva. As his question was being ignored he stood close behind Susan and leaned down to make sure he was being heard, "Obviously not." Susan could smell his beery breath, "I think what you need is a nice shoulder massage."

"Please don't touch me," Susan said icily .

"Leave her alone!" John stood up knocking his chair over. The interloper began massaging Susan's shoulders. "And just what are you going to do if I don't leave her alone?.... I think she rather likes it don't you?" Four of his equally revolting companions had now joined him and amused themselves by leering into the faces of Susan and John. Susan looked at John and winked as she spoke calmly. "It's rather good actually." She lifted her left hand over her right shoulder and reached out to grasp the stranger's fingers, "Am I allowed to see the face of the man with the magic hands?" She stood up slowly, still holding on with her left hand, turned round and forced herself to look into the grinning sweaty face of her molester. Then, almost within the same second, she jerked his little finger back so that it cracked and brought her knee sharply up into his groin. With her other hand she rammed the handle of a dessert spoon deep into his left nostril and held onto it as he fell to the ground with a scream of agony. She knelt beside him. "Now, let me tell you what's going to happen next..... no don't move or I'll do this..." He screamed again as she twisted the spoon, "What's your name first of all?"

"Craig."

"Well Craig it's most important that you don't move. Just lie perfectly still and we'll get you some help." To John she said, "will you talk to the landlord and ask him to call an ambulance. .... Ah, here he is already."

A thin young man with a worried expression hurried onto the scene shouting at the waitress to call an ambulance. He asked Susan what happened.

"I'm not absolutely sure," she said sweetly as she stood up, "He came over to our table to entertain us with some kind of trick with cutlery but it seemed to go horribly wrong and he tripped and fell on the spoon, poor man. No, don't touch him. If you pull it out he could well bleed to death." John glanced at the small group of people that had gathered. The injured man's companions had melted away into the night. The others had obviously seen everything that had happened but made no attempt to protest at Susan's version of events. She stood up and said to the manager, "I'm afraid we must go straight away. We have to pick up our children at nine o'clock."

"Would you mind leaving your name and telephone number - just in case he becomes - er seriously ill."

"Of course," said Susan writing on a beermat, "I'm Louise Walker and this is my husband Peter. This is my number and that's our address in Luton. ....Poor chap. I'm a trained nurse and I've given him some first aid. He'll probably be all right. He also seems to have broken one of his fingers as he fell. See how it is sticking out a funny angle? Just get him to lie still till the ambulance arrives and it's best if he doesn't try to speak."

Just after they stepped out into the cool night air a siren announced the arrival of an ambulance outside the pub. Then, walking quickly up the slight hill that led to Herbert Street they heard another siren and looked back to see a car arrive and two uniformed policemen get out and hurry into the restaurant bar. John and Susan sat down on the low wall which surrounded the tiny garden in front of number one Herbert Street. Everything was bathed in orange light from a lamp post on the opposite pavement and now all was silent apart from the faint sound of an aeroplane taking off from Luton .

"Do you think they will come after us?" said John, slightly out of breath.

"No. Not unless someone saw as walking up here. Why would they anyway?"

"Someone must have called the police. Maybe the manager knows what really happened."

"Don't worry, they won't be able to trace us. You paid cash remember?"

"And who are Peter and Louise Walker? I suppose they don't exist either."

"Actually they do," It was Susan's turn to pause for breath, "They used to run a care home for old people and they were cruel and abusive to the inmates - one of them was my friend's grandmother. There wasn't enough evidence to convict them but they were forced to retire early. They now live in Luton - after getting away with murder - almost literally. I gave the landlord their real address and phone number. I drop them in it every now and then. It's great fun."

"I'm impressed with your er - self defence skills - first

42

aid I think you called it. I would have done my bit, though, if you'd given me the chance."

"I know you would," she leant against him so he could put his arm round her, "There's nothing lacking in your courage but I didn't need you to be a hero. I took over because he and his friends would have badly injured you, and then me as well probably, and I'm damn sure the other customers wouldn't have come to help. I don't blame them. I always try to avoid confrontation and violence."

"What do you call that then!"

"I wasn't confrontational. He assaulted me if you remember. I just used reasonable force to defuse the situation. He'll be fine in a couple of days." She lifted her legs onto the wall and laid her head on John's lap to look up at the sky. "What are you thinking?"

"I was thinking that you remind me of when I worked in an African animal rescue centre and I used to cuddle a female lion cub who would lie on me just like you are - staring at the stars. She carried on doing that until she was too grown up for it to be safe. Then one day, purring madly, she reached up with her paw and scratched me under the chin. Quite deep cuts they were. Look, you can still see the scars."

"Lift your chin up, I can't see... oh yes!.. What was she called, this other woman of yours- shameless hussy."

"Chloe. Anyway she was beautiful and dangerous at the same time, like you."

"I'm not dangerous I promise you," Susan sat up and put her face close to John's and looked into his eyes. "I mean it. I hate aggression. I'm just protective of myself and other people that I like. Actually I've never hurt anyone before - ever. Well, only my self-defence trainer when I was in the army and that was an accident. 'Come at me hard as you like-give it all you've got,' he said, but I don't think he was quite ready poor man.."

"You were in the army?"

"Army nurse, yes, but we all learnt survival skills as well."

"I believe you – but excuse me you don't look butch enough. I mean where are your bulging muscles? You have the figure of a teenager."

"Thank you kind sir. Listen, I want you to understand something. You probably would agree that I'm not exactly ugly and unappealing to men, yes?"

"And you're so modest too."

"I'm being serious. Well, people often think that it must be great to be attractive, or beautiful or sexy or whatever. Well it's not always wonderful. Men seem to come in two categories. There are the ones who try it on all the time without considering the possibility they might be not be wanted. They seem to think that the mere fact that they are attracted to you somehow makes them appealing. Then there are the ones who find attractive women threatening in some way and go all shy and can't even talk to you properly. They're the worst. They're useless. I hate shyness. God, I must sound awful - but it's true -I can't help it."

"Is that why women often seem so relaxed talking to gay men?"

"Probably. I suppose it's the other side of the coin. You don't have to 'perform' as an 'attractive' person. You feel nice and safe."

"Do we talk properly?"

"Yes. Good innit? Anyway when I was a teenager unwanted attention became quite a problem. I used to think how nice it would be, just now and again, to wear something like a burqa, so people would have no idea whether you were ugly or beautiful and just talk to you as the person you really are. Don't worry, I've given up on the idea! So, yes, you're right, I didn't grow big muscles in the army but remember I never said I did unarmed combat and ten mile hikes carrying fifty kilo sacks. I loved learning survival skills best of all. Everyone should do it. Never mind your Karate and your Tai Quan tiddley pom whatever. Knowing what do do in horrible situations is worth millions. Take threes, for instance."

"Threes."

"Yes threes. Look, suppose you survive an aeroplane crash and you are miles from anywhere and you want to signal where you are, just keep doing three of something. A single thing no-one notices, two of something could be a coincidence, but not three things. If you are in the jungle light three fires if you can. If you are in the wilderness keep putting groups of three rocks together leading to wherever you are. My grandfather, when he was fighting in Burma, was on a mission to rescue five of his comrades who had been captured and taken into the jungle. They were resting by a small mountain stream when they noticed that it suddenly stopped flowing for about a minute, three times in a row, and then another three times. So his patrol followed the river upstream till they came to a soldier whose leg was badly wounded. The enemy had left him for dead in the jungle but he had managed crawl to the stream where the water rushed through a narrow gap between to large rocks. He found a plank from a broken bridge and had summoned up enough strength to use it to hold back the water and let it go again. He told them that the enemy and the prisoners were upstream and his friends were soon rescued by the patrol. After that everyone called him Damplank. He became a great friend of my grandad and when I was very young I remember him coming to visit. I always thought his name was Dan Plank."

"OK. Threes. If I turn up on Sunday with three hats on my head you'll know there's a bomb in my suitcase and I'm being forced to blow myself up on your doorstep."

"Do you want to come in for a bit?"

John stood up. "I really want to but I'd better go. I have to go home, get my camera gear and be ready for an early start in the morning."

"Where is home? You never told me."

"Watford. My mate's house. Before then it was a ship, my home I mean, not the house - but that's another story. What are you going to be doing?"

"I'm estate-agenting tomorrow and then Saturday I'm going to my friend's hen night in the evening. I don't get drunk and get hangovers so come round on Sunday morning at nine o'clock please. Here's the key to the back door so if I'm not up you can wake me." She put her arms round John's neck and kissed him, "I'll be ready for you." She opened her front door and from the extra height given her by the doorstep, turned and kissed him again on his forehead. "Good night."

John struck a pose in the middle of the street, "Good night. Parting is such sweet sorrow that I shall say good night until the morrow."

"Who said that."

"I did."

"Oh. Ha, bloody ha."

"Juliet said it to Romeo."

"Then I should have said it."

"Yes you should."

"You daft bugger. Go home to Watford."

"And get ye to a nunnery."

"Shut up," said Susan as John walked away carrying his leather folder and swinging his other arm. Susan slammed her door and opened it again. "I love you," she shouted. John stopped and swung round on one foot but before he could answer an upstairs window opened further down the street, "And Romeo loves you an' all. Now if you both shut up we might be able to get some bleedin' sleep."

Chapter Seven

John Meets Ben

The Gazette building stood on the same shopping parade as the estate agent offices where John had met Susan the previous day. It was about a hundred metres closer to the town centre and set back from the road to accommodate an overcrowded car park in front of the building. John parked in the street, hoisted his huge camera bag onto his shoulder and went in. Minutes later he found himself in the busy newsroom where the editor introduced him to the sub editor, news editor, chief reporter and the eight other reporters. There were no photographers.

"One's on holiday, the other is having his appendix out. That's why you are here," explained the editor. John looked into the faces of everyone as he was introduced. They varied a great deal in their ages and physique but all seemed very friendly. Dick East, the news editor, showed him to the photographer's corner, made sure he was familiar with the computer set-up and brought him a coffee. "OK. Here is the diary with your jobs for today and Saturday. There is a lot of stuff as you can see. I've marked the priority jobs with a "P" in red. The others, well do them if you can. If you can't get to them don't worry. It's much more important that you get good pictures from the main ones. There are usually too many things to photograph and not enough time - like every other newspaper in the country, but you can see I've left some gaps so you have time to load your pictures into our system – and eat as well! Today's first job is not until ten o'clock so take your time. Saturday's not too busy during the day but the main event is in the evening. It's the start of the Hemel Spectacular which is a whole fortnight of events. It's being held in a big marquee in the Boxmoor end of town, between the church, the cricket ground and the canal."

"I saw them putting it up," said John, "It's huge, bigger than a circus tent."

"You'll need these, a ticket to get in and this back-stage pass. Here are the numbers to press to open our main office door in case you want to get in here after normal hours. We're hoping to use at least ten photographs in the centre pages and one on the front. It will be dead easy to get pictures because it will all happen just in front of you. Do what you want but there are two very important shots. The first one will be of the mayor unveiling the display case with the skeleton of the mystery woman in it."

"Oh yes. I've heard of that. The dead highway woman or Mrs. Snook or whoever she is."

"Make sure Dr. Salter the archaeologist is in the picture. Also Ben Carter if you can get him. He's the man who dug the skeleton up but he's a very retiring sort of chap and we haven't been able to get a shot of him yet. The other must-have picture is the Great Zoldini. Have you heard of him?" John shook his head, "Neither have I. Apparently he is a world famous magician who does spectacular illusions and his stunt will be the grand climax to the evening. I can't stand magic shows myself."

"OK-got all that."

"Oh. Just one more thing. After the unveiling don't bother to get any more pictures of the Mayor, Daphne Mallacott. She's in the paper often enough."

One of the reporters interrupted, "She is also real cow and pig ignorant. We all call her Mayor Malaprop because she can't even make one of her crap speeches without getting the words wrong. Only yesterday she opened a school garden and started talking about 'orgasmic vegetables'."

The editor chipped in,"Sometimes I'm tempted to publish what she says word for word-but even I am not that cruel."

Half an hour later John found himself on his first assignment - to illustrate the lack of water in the River Gade. He was to meet a concerned resident in the park by the old iron bridge over the river. He had been told it was in easy walking distance so he left his bag in the car and travelled light, carrying just one camera fitted with his favourite all-purpose wide-angle lens. As he came near the bridge he could see a solitary figure leaning on the white-painted railings and gazing into the water. She was a middle-aged woman in an anorak and green Wellingtons. She didn't seem to be aware of his approach and kept staring downwards. John was just about to cough when she began speaking without looking up,"You must be the Gazette man. I've been waiting half an hour."

"I'm sorry, they told me ten o'clock."

"I'm sure they did," she said in a voice like a headmistress, "Don't apologise - those reporters, they get everything wrong. I'm Molly Waring," she said, turning to look at him at last, "Come and see what I'm on about."

"You're saying there's not enough water in the river."

"Well look at it."

"Mmm. There's a lot of weeds."

"That is part of the problem but this time last year the water was right up to the banks on either side and this is after all that winter rainfall we've had. The level has gone down about a metre in the last month. Something strange is happening because now you can walk right across the river bed."

"Would you mind standing in the middle of the river for me?"

"No, don't get me in the photograph. I hate having my picture taken."

"Oh, it's all right. It'll be mostly river. I just need a distant figure to illustrate the size of the problem." She still looked reluctant but followed John down to the river edge. He showed her the camera, "I can let you see the pictures on the screen when we've finished and you can tell me what you think." He held her hand as she cautiously stepped into the clear water and found firm footing on the pebbles. "If you are OK there I'm going back up onto the bridge." By the time he got there she was in the middle of the river with the water lapping at the top of her boots.

"There you are," she said, "You couldn't have done this last year, not since the drought of 1976, but I don't suppose you remember that."

"I wasn't even born then but my parents told me about it. Right, if you're ready just look at me. That's it. Only don't smile. It's a serious subject I think."

"Yes it is, and I hate this. I'm no good in front of a camera."

"You're doing very well. I've nearly finished."

Just one more picture. Can you put your arms out to the side-like this."

"Why?"

"It tells the reader that the story is less about you but more about what's around you."

"Like this."

"Yes, but don't smile. Just talk to me. It will relax you."

"What shall I say?"

"Just count to ten."

"… five, six, seven..."

"OK finished. I'll come and help you out." On the way down he fired off a couple of shots of her wading through the water which he later decided were by far the best pictures. He thanked her for being so helpful and was very happy when she looked at the camera screen and approved the images.

Walking back to his car he noticed a transparent plastic bag stuck to the windscreen containing a piece of paper on which he could see printed in red letters 'DOCUMENTS ENCLOSED.' 'Oh shit, shit, shit,' he thought, 'It must be over an hour, I suppose.' He ripped it off the windscreen and tore it open. In bold red lettering it said;

Hemel Hempstead Parking Control

It is an offence to leave a vehicle in this parking bay for more than one hour. The driver of this vehicle is now liable to a fine of £60 payable within fourteen days.

...and then on a second sheet of paper -

NOT REALLY!

WELCOME TO THE GAZETTE!!

John heard a loud cheering and whistling. He looked up and saw a gaggle of reporters waving at him from the upstairs windows of the Gazette building. His mobile phone went off, "Oh very funny!" he said looking up at a grinning Dick East with a phone to his ear.

"You've passed the initiation ceremony," chortled Dick, "I'm sure you're greatly relieved and, some more good news - your next job is cancelled. Are you coming back up?"

"No," said John, pretending to be really offended, "I shall resign immediately and never speak to any of you again. Seriously, I'm going to take a trip up the river. The lady on the bridge says there is plenty of water upstream. It's worth a look I think. Is that all right?"

"Sure. But don't get carried away. You've got all those other jobs this afternoon."

"I'll be fine - as long as I don't get any more parking tickets."

Taking the main road north out of town along the Gade Valley it took him about fifteen minutes to find the meadow where the river started as a mere trickle of water. He drove back the way he came, glancing now and then at the stream as it more or less followed the same direction as the road. He stopped on a bridge less than a mile from the town where the river seemed very healthy indeed with a great volume of water flowing between its banks. He parked his car and walked beside the river for a while until it disappeared into a thick wood which was overgrown with elder trees and brambles. It was impossible to go any further so he returned to the car and drove about a quarter of a mile closer to town where he found a gap in the trees which revealed a rough track, hardly more than a path. He drove his car onto the grass verge and walked down the track. He had put on his green camouflage jacket and carried a pair of binoculars as well as his camera so that he would look like a birdwatcher. The wood was so thick John felt as if he was walking through a tunnel and he had to bend down in quite a few places to avoid the branches. He soon came to a junction with a larger 'tunnel' through which the river flowed. The path turned sharply to the right and continued along the river bank with just enough room for one person to walk. Alcoves had been cut into the undergrowth which he presumed were passing places should anyone meet an oncoming pedestrian. John observed that the canopy of twigs and small branches had been carefully cut back over the path but over the water the trees were untouched. Many years of growth had turned the old and twisted branches into fantastic shapes, many of them festooned with moss and creepers. He was pleasantly surprised to see the bright blue flash of a kingfisher as it skimmed along the water before disappearing into the trees. Then, quite suddenly after a sharp bend, the river opened up into a lagoon of almost still water about the size of a tennis court. As he became quite overwhelmed by the magical beauty of the trees reflected in the water a sudden noise broke the silence. He remained rooted to the spot as the sound of rushing water, quiet at first and then louder and louder, jolted him out of his trance. He glanced upstream to see if it was coming from there but immediately realised it was in the other direction at the far end of the lagoon. Minutes later he found himself climbing round the edge of a dam consisting of a wall of interlocking steel shutters similar to those he had seen on large construction sites. It soon became obvious to him that the sudden noise occurred because the water had just begun to flow over a low point in the centre of the dam. He could also see that it fell vertically five metres down to a waterwheel which was turning merrily.

"Can I help you?" The question came from a sixty year old man standing at the foot of the dam with a large adjustable spanner in his hand. John could feel himself going red in the face as he apologised, "I'm really sorry - intruding on your private space. I know I shouldn't be here. I'll go straight away."

"Would you mind telling me why you've come?"

"I'm a photographer with the Gazette. We are doing a story about the lack of water in the River Gade."

"Ah."

"I'd better go. Once again I do apologise."

"No. Wait. I want to talk to you." There was a loud clunk as he threw the spanner on top of some others in a large tool bag. "You'd better come down. There are some steps behind you, see them?" He turned his back on John and ambled over to the veranda of the nearby house and slumped down in the rocking chair. John followed him across the grassy clearing towards the strange house. On the way he found it impossible to stop himself staring at the weird pieces of machinery lying around.

"Do you want a beer?" The older man lifted a can from a cool box by his feet and waved it in the air.

"No thanks. I won't even have one drink if I'm driving."

"Where's your car?"

"It's beside the road where I came in at the end of your path." There was an uncomfortable pause. John tried to look as relaxed as possible, leaning against the rail of the veranda and looking up at the dam. He was uncertain how to behave and felt it would be prudent to leave his new companion in his own personal space. "I'm John Street, by the way."

"I know who you are. Do you know who I am?"

"No."

"Susan told me all about you. You're buying her house."

"Ah! You must be Ben. She's buying your house."

"She is... if you mean what you say, that is."

"Oh yes, I'm going to buy hers, and if you want proof of my good intentions she will be passing a decent amount of money on to you as a deposit from money I've already put into her bank account. And," he said gaining confidence and stepping onto the veranda, "there is also the question of whether you mean what you say."

The older man smiled for the first time since John's arrival, "All right. All right. Listen, Susan thinks you're something pretty wonderful. So I can assume you can't be all that bad." He stood up and held out his hand, "I'm Ben Carter. Pleased to meet you, John - or should I say Herbert." John shook his hand and laughed, "She really has told you everything!" He made a sweeping gesture, "Is this what she's buying, all of...of ...... this?"

"Yes. All four acres of it. Didn't she tell you?"

"No. I didn't ask, and we just didn't get round to discussing it. I don't think it's one of her secrets, unlike her second job."

"Well I'm not going to tell you what she does for a living but don't worry about it, she's not doing anything sinister."

"She'll tell me when she's ready I expect but I don't care, it's none of my business I suppose - like your house."

"She won't mind me telling you all about this place. She asked me this morning if she could show you round on Sunday afternoon. I'll tell her you're here," he said picking up his phone from a shelf behind his head.

"No don't do that. She might think I have been nosing into her affairs..." Ben raised his palm and shook his head as he dialled a number.

"Hello, this is Ben. Guess who I met this morning ….a friend of yours....out taking photographs of the River Gade...... yes... John... well I ought to be able to spot a newspaper photographer by now. Anyway I've invited him to have a look round my place. Hope you don't mind. You can still bring him over on Sunday and we can have a chat then. Do you want to speak to him? …... Ok I'll tell him. ….Bye." He put the phone back on the shelf. "She's with a client but she says she's very happy we've met and wants me to show you round. So..." he said, getting up.

"Lead the way," said John, "Have you known Susan long?"

"About six months. I met her in the estate agent's when I decided sell this place. It never got as far as the company sales list because she wanted to buy it. Apparently she used to play here as a child, long before the house was built, and had often dreamt of living here. I had the place valued and her offer was about right. I won't have to pay agents' fees either - neither will she when you buy her place. She's not daft is she?"

"Oh no, you're right there."

Twenty minutes later they had completed the tour of the property and now stood in front of the dam where they had first met. Ben was just summing up his situation. "So there you are. It'll all have to be flattened by bulldozers pretty soon. I might have been able to get a bit more money by selling to developers but it's not going to be worth millions. There is only planning permission for a single dwelling. Mind you if that cow Mallacott and her friends get hold of it you never know what might happen. It might end up as a housing estate. I'd rather die than sell it to her. No I want Susan to have it. I know she won't ruin it like they would."

"What's going to happen to the dam?"

"Oh, you mean the garden water feature?" he grinned and looked sideways at John, "That's staying. It just happens to supply my modest requirements of electrical power as well as being decorative."

"Am I right in thinking that this is the reason for the drop in the water level in the river?"

"Might be."

"It's very low in the park and the lake in the town centre is almost dried up."

"OK. See that sluice gate over there. That normally allows the full amount of water to flow past the dam when I'm working on it. I've been making the wall a bit higher so I can get more power. I finished the work two weeks ago and closed the sluice almost completely so the dam would fill up. I didn't think anyone would notice."

"As far as I know only one person did. I just photographed her standing in the middle of the river."

"Well, as you may of observed when you arrived, it's full now and has just started spilling over the top of the wall, so from now on the river should be flowing normally all through the town."

"Good."

"Are you going to tell the paper about this?"

"You'd rather I didn't, obviously," John walked off a little way while he thought about it, "Well it won't be much of a story now the water level is going to rise again."

"Tell you what. You forget about finding this place and I'll let you on to the site when they come to knock the house down. How about that."

"Are you going to be here to the last then."

"Don't know what I'm going to do to be doing to be honest. I suppose you want me to throw myself in front of the bulldozers."

"Of course."

"Did I tell you I used to be a snapper for the national papers, in London? Fleet Street it was then."

"No."

"Another time, perhaps."

"It's all right, I won't tell the paper anything about the dam."

"Thank you."

"Will Susan be able to get electricity?"

"No chance. Not unless she pays about £30,000, there are no cables anywhere near here. I'm hoping the bastards won't take the dam to pieces. She's probably going to need it."

"Oh now I understand why she said she would have to do a lot of work on the property and also how she is able to afford somewhere to live on four acres of land. Listen, I had better go. Thank you very much for showing me everything."

"Nice to meet you and I want you to know how happy it's made me showing you around. I don't do this with many people."

"I feel privileged."

Ben's face became very sad suddenly, "I'm going to be heartbroken having to leave all this." He watched as John began climbing back up the steps, "See you on Sunday."

"I'll see you before then on Saturday evening when I'm

supposed to photograph you with the mystery skeleton, and Dr. Salter and the mayor."

"If you want a picture of me you'll have to do it when she's gone to the toilet or something."

Back at the Gazette office Dick East asked him how he got on.

"Nothing really. The river seems to be flowing quite well north of the town and I met an old man who seemed certain that it would be back to normal in a few days."

"Was it Ben Carter?"

"Yes it was. You don't seem surprised."

Dick laughed, "He's been in our paper many times, mainly about disputes with the council over his weird property, arguments with the mayor in particular." He tapped the open diary with his pen, "Are you going to be all right with these jobs? I recommend that you download your stuff as often as possible. Now, as soon as you have got enough pictures on Saturday evening come back here and leave the camera card on the editor's desk. He will be coming in about nine o'clock to make up the early pages so he will download your images then. He will be at the opening with the V.I.Ps so you won't need to leave caption details. He knows everybody anyway."

"Thank you I'll be fine. As for now I'll give you the first images of Molly Waring on the bridge, then I'll grab a sandwich and be off on the other stuff."

He found himself enjoying the newsroom banter as he worked on his images. A reporter hurried into the room and clicked the remote control for the big internet display screen at the end of the room, "I just heard on the car radio that the Home Secretary has been in a hunting accident in Scotland." He turned to face his colleagues, "Yes. He was shot in the Cairngorms apparently."

"Sounds very nasty," said the editor without looking up.

Then someone with a strong Welsh accent spoke up, "I went to Loch Lomond in January. Bloody cold it was too. I got frostbite in the Trossachs."There was a chorus of groans.

Six hours later John found himself in the pedestrian area of the town centre attending the last job of the day. By then he had photographed a hundred year old spinster, a retiring headmistress, a school netball match, father and son marathon runners, a little boy with learning difficulties -who insisted on taking everything out of his camera bag, a cat who had been shot with an air gun and now he was about to photograph an unveiling of a statue in the town centre by Mayor Daphne Mallacott. As she introduced herself he noticed that she smelt of cheap perfume and had lipstick on her teeth. She then told him to make sure he had some film in his camera which caused her companions to laugh politely. Encouraged by this she said,"And I hope you have insurance, I wouldn't want my face to crack your lens!" John's head filled with very impolite replies but, like many others around him he fixed a meaningless smile on his face and said nothing.

The statue was hidden under a grey cloth which was loosely held in place with a cord at the end of which dangled a tassel ready for the mayor to pull. About twenty people stood round in a circle. A few of these were trying to look at their watches without being noticed.

"Madam Mayor if you're ready...." said the sculptor, a red faced man in a brown suit who was very good at fawning. The mayor stepped forward and brought out a sheaf of papers.

'Oh no!, ' thought John, 'we could be here for ages!'

He endured his suffering by his usual way of slipping into daydreams. He thought of Susan. *'I wonder what she is doing now. Not out with her hen night pals - that's tomorrow. One thing's for certain, I'm not going to spend much time worrying about her. She seems quite capable of looking after herself.'* He smiled as he thought of her tactics in the pub, *'I'd better be careful not get on the wrong side of her and if I do I'm damn sure I'm going to avoid physical confrontation. I like the giant bed though - and the things you can do on it! How did the rest of the room get wrecked? Oh now I remember......'*

"… and now it gives me great pleasure," John shook off his day dream and stepped forward, camera at the ready, "to unveil this statue of Henry the Eighth, which I am sure will be enjoyed by all the people of Hemel Hempstead, and our visitors of course, who I hope will stop by here and admire.... and admire...." The mayor tugged hard on the cord but nothing happened. The sculptor ran round the statue, fiddled with something and came back, "That should do it. Allow me assist you Madam Mayor." They stood in readiness as John got into position and took a couple of 'before' shots. "After three then," said the mayor, "One, two three, pull!" Nothing happened. The tiny crowd surged forward and many hands grabbed the cord and the edges of the cloth. "Heave!" said everyone, and they heaved. There was a sound of tearing cloth followed by a grinding crunch as the whole party fell to the ground with the cloth on top of them. The last to be uncovered was the mayor who sat pointing at the top of the statue with a trembling and dusty finger. "Look! She shouted with a quavering voice. It's got no head! Someone's decastrated it."

"There it is," said the sculptor, pointing to a place

between the mayor's legs from where the stern bearded face of Henry looked back at his body. Minutes later John walked to his car, put his camera bag in the boot and headed home to Watford.

"Those are the best pictures I've taken in a long time," he said to himself, "They're going to love me at the Gazette."

Half an hour later he staggered up the stairs to his room and dumped his camera bag by his bed. He carried his supper, a takeaway vegetable curry, down to the kitchen and was relieved to see a note from his flatmate telling him that he had gone away for the week-end. John liked to eat alone and do the crossword at the same time when he was tired. Susan had left him a message on his phone, "Hello Herbert Street this is Susan Savage, your lover. I like saying that. It seems so honest and sounds just the tiniest bit sort of improper, unlike sweetheart or darling or dearest. Anyway I miss you lots. I think of you all the time. At work today they kept asking me why I was smiling. Apparently I'm usually very stern unless I'm talking to a customer. I must be in love. I'm going to sleep now because I have a busy day tomorrow. It's a quarter to ten. Goodnight. By the way you haven't said you love me yet. It's all right, I know you do. I just want you to say it. Er.., I'm not going to say it now either just so you know how it feels." Then another message, "Oh, bugger it. I love you."

John pressed the recall button to be told, "This number is not responding. The telephone you are trying to reach may be switched off. Please try later."

"Okay. I'll do just that," he mumbled as he felt his eyelids closing on him, but he didn't. He only just managed to shower and clean his teeth before falling asleep seconds after climbing into bed.

Chapter Eight

Hemel Spectacular

Saturday was less busy for John with a village horticultural society show, a group of four cyclists wanting sponsors for their ride to Paris and a football match in the afternoon. There were enough gaps between jobs to go into the office and download the day's photographs as well as those from the day before. This pleased him because he wanted to empty his camera and have a rest so as to be ready for the great event in the evening. He was still missing Susan a lot. He thought himself lucky that the day's jobs were fascinating enough to fully occupy his mind. He loved the flower show. He couldn't recall ever being to one before. There were row upon row of perfect flowers in green conical metal vases on white paper-covered tables, bright green cabbages bigger than footballs and sweet peas with huge petals, too heavy for their stalks, in pastel shades of pink and blue. The pictures seemed to leap into his camera with very little effort on his part. His best photographs were of the ancient and weathered old men carrying parsnips almost a metre long and giant carrots with skins the same colour and texture as their owners. He wished Susan was with him to share the experience. Like people who yearn for a missing close relative, he seemed see her everywhere. During the football in the afternoon he was so sure that he saw her in the crowd that at half time he walked to where he thought she was sitting. Before he got up close to the woman in a white T-shirt with straight blond hair like Susan's he realised his mistake and changed course to the tea hut. *'What's the matter with me?'* he thought, *'I'm going to be with her in less than 24 hours so why am I feeling so anxious?'*

His mobile phone went off during the very boring second half of the match but it was just Dick East from the Gazette telling him that he was going himself to the Hemel Spectacular and would be on hand if John wanted any help.

After nipping back to the flat for food and to shower and change into a smart suit, John lay on his bed and tried to phone Susan again only to be met with the usual answer phone message. *"Well, time to go. I'm going to have enough to think about for the next few hours. I had better forget all desires of the body and soul and concentrate on what I'm doing."*

He arrived at the mammoth tent very early at six o'clock, an hour before the principal guests were due to arrive. Dick East met him straight away looking uncomfortably smart in dinner jacket and black bow tie and grinning amiably.

"Hello," said John, "You're early."

"So are you. I got the time wrong. What's your excuse?"

"I always arrive early to things like this to size-up the situation and plan what I'm going to do."

"Ah. That's probably a good move on your part because there is a bit of a snag. The Great Zoldini's henchmen have said with great forcefulness that there is to be no photography during his act. So you won't be allowed inside the tent during any part of the performance, which is a bit of a shame really because I'm told it's going to be quite an amazing trick. That fenced-off area down the other end is the Great Zoldini's territory. You can see his personal gorillas standing round it to keep people away."

John looked puzzled, "I wonder why he doesn't want any photographs."

"Maybe he's worried that we might be able to see how it's done and publish pictures of his secret."

"As if we would!"

"Quite. As if.."

"What are you smiling at anyway?

"Oh. It's just these occasions. They always end up as a farce but then what would we do if we didn't have something to laugh at on a Saturday night? It should be rather fun. See you later."

John examined his surroundings. It was a huge area with thirty tables set at a short distance from the performance area. These were meant to accommodate the dignitaries, their guests and others who had paid for the more expensive tickets. There was standing room for everyone else but it was quite apparent they would have a good view of the proceedings due to the natural slope of the land on which the tent stood. There was no raised platform on the performance area, just a surface of interlocking boards laid directly onto the turf. At the back of this stage were black curtains to the left and ten metre square paper screens to the left and right. Located a short distance from the tent entrance on the left hand side was a long Perspex box containing skeletal remains. John made an examination, *'So this is her,'* he thought to himself as he lifted his camera, *'Good job there's plenty of light. I wouldn't get much using a flash with that Perspex.'* He lowered his camera again because he was suddenly overwhelmed with sadness, *'This isn't right. She shouldn't be on display like a fairground freak even if she was a criminal. She was someone's daughter, sister maybe, even a mother - and supposing she was innocent. There's no proof she was guilty of anything......'*

He could hear voices behind him. One was Ben Carter. "Hello John." John turned round to see Ben advancing towards him and carrying a large white sheet. Walking beside him was a distinguished man in his thirties.

"This is Dr. Salter," said Ben, "Doctor, this is John Street who works for the Gazette."

"Pleased to meet you," said John, "can I get a photograph of the two of you with the skeleton?"

"With pleasure," said Dr. Salter, "You're just in time. We're just about to cover it up ready for it to be uncovered again later by the mayor."

"Thanks. It makes my job so much easier if I get some of the shots in the bag nice and early. And I want a close-up shot with just you two and the box."

"I understand. I know Ben doesn't want to be photographed with the mayor at the unveiling - and why. It's all right, I can't stand the woman either but I've got to be there to say a few words after she performs."

When John had finished he asked Dr. Salter for his first name for the picture caption.

"It had better be Gerald for the paper," he said, giving John his card, "you call me Gerry please." He took John's card in return and smiled, "Herbert Street of Herbert Street. Is that your real name? Ben just called you John."

"Herbert's my middle name. You can call me by my

first name which is John. I'm buying number one Herbert Street just for the address."

"I hope you've told the Gazette. They'd like that."

They managed to cover up the skeleton with a few minutes to spare as people began to arrive. John watched them intently. This was his first opportunity to scrutinise large numbers of Hemel Hempstead people at close quarters. He loved scrutinising people. He was rather surprised how much these ones varied in size, shape, age, health and attractiveness. He also was surprised how friendly they all seemed to be and how so many took the trouble to make him feel welcome. He shuddered as he remembered covering the opening of a sports complex at a town in a neighbouring county a few weeks before. There they tried to order him about as if he was one of their servants and were downright rude to anyone who was old, disabled or dark-skinned. Not so with these people. Several of them made a point of asking who he was and what had happened to the usual Gazette photographers. Many times he explained that one of the usual photographers was on holiday and the other was recovering from an illness. "I'm afraid you will just have to put up with the rubbish photographer for now," he joked. The audience area was filling up quickly now apart from two of the tables near the front which remained empty. "Who's going to sit there?" he asked an aged toastmaster standing resplendent in his scarlet tail coat, red face, flowing white hair and matching handlebar moustache.

"You must be from the Gazette. These seats are for the mayor and other dignitaries. After everyone else has arrived they will proceed down the main aisle and onto the stage for the opening ceremony. After that the mayor and Dr. Salter will walk back up the aisle to unveil the skeleton and finally we have the Great Zoldini doing whatever he does." His voice sounded very disapproving at this point and he looked at John with half-closed eyelids peering over half-rimmed glasses.

'I bet he's going to call me 'dear boy' any moment now,' thought John and then spoke aloud "Well I'm not allowed to take pictures of that last bit."

"Lucky you. You can go home early. I've got to stay to the bitter end."

"Thanks," said John, "You've been very helpful."

"Not at all, dear boy. Not at all. Always like to help a fellow sufferer."

John wandered back up the aisle to the entrance to be ready for the procession to arrive. On the way he found himself becoming anxious again, very similar to his experience earlier in the day when he thought he saw Susan in the football crowd. Once again he thought he saw her, this time half hidden in the audience on the far side of the seating area. He was about to make his way over there but whoever it was had disappeared from view. *'Why do I keep I feeling like this?'* he asked himself rather crossly, *'I'm in love with the most amazing, beautiful and mysterious woman I could ever expect to meet so why do I feel so anxious about her? I bet it's because I got all upset about the skeleton - made me realise that everyone is vulnerable, even Susan. I couldn't bear it if anything were to happen to her. Which is natural I suppose. I must really love her. She wants me to tell her that as well. I wish she hadn't asked me to say it. It's going to sound all rehearsed and unreal now. I should have said it first. She is going to get annoyed soon I can tell. But what am I going to do? Buy roses and stuff and have an orchestra playing ... I'd feel like a prat... I AM being a prat NOW actually. Nothing is going to happen to her.'* "Snap out of it John Street – Herbert- whatever my name is, and get on with the job in hand."

"That's a good idea!" laughed Dick East."

John realised he had said the last sentence out loud, "Sorry, talking to myself again."

"It's OK. It's just that if you are thinking of snapping out of it now is just the right moment." The toastmaster was standing right beside them. He rang a large hand bell, threw it to the ground and cupped his hands round his mouth. "MY LORDS, LADIEEEEES AND GENTLEMEN PLEASE BE UPSTANDING FOR HER WORSHIP THE MAYOR, COUNCILLOR MRS. DAPHNE MALLACOTT AND THE PARADE!!!" Powerful spotlights lit up entrance. John looked for Susan again but it was too dark to see anyone in the audience. Everyone turned towards the entrance as a marching brass band started up outside. John's mobile phone rang, "Hello John it's me, Susan, can you talk?"

"Not really - I mean only for about thirty seconds. It's going to get very noisy in a moment. Listen. It's so good to hear your voice. I miss you so much and it's only been two days."

"Miss you too. You sound as if you're really busy."

"I am a bit!" shouted John as the brass band reached the entrance very noisily. "I'll see you in the morning!"

"OK. I didn't want you to think I'd forgotten you..." Both their voices were drowned by the music. John swapped the phone for his camera just in time as the parade entered the tent onto the massive red carpet. His mood now swung from anxiety to a warm glow of happiness and he wondered at the effect of a few spoken words on his soul. He was now able give his full attention to the scene unfolding before him. The band was closely followed by a score of majorettes who were showered with so much silver tape no-one noticed how many battens they dropped. Then there were the clowns, some on three-metre stilts who dropped balloons and confetti on the crowd. After they all had passed right through the tent and out through the back of the stage there was a moment of silence before the mace-bearer appeared followed by the mayor in full regalia, various councillors and their guests. The mayor tottered with great difficulty down the red carpet on her high heels accompanied by a deathly hush until the noble toastmaster started clapping loudly. This encouraged enough polite applause from the front ranks of the audience to enable her and her guests to get to their seats without too much embarrassment. The applause was increased tenfold with the addition of loud cheering as the fifty-two members of the combined choir of Hemel Hempstead schools walked in carrying lighted candles. As soon as they were all inside they stopped while everyone waited expectantly. Several of the younger choristers exchanged smiles and waves with parents while the older ones stared straight ahead as if they had no knowledge of any living relative. Two burly sixth-formers came to the front, knelt on one knee and each put an arm round the other's shoulder. The young woman conductor, a music teacher from the largest school in the town, stepped forward, climbed to the top of this human podium and sat down. The boys stood up ready to march forward with their precious load who was now facing the opposite direction towards her choir. She gingerly reached down and took her baton from the toastmaster. There was laughter and more cheering as the two boys pretended to stumble which luckily the conductor also thought was funny. Then she held out her hands palm-downwards to appeal for silence and raised her baton as the two boys stood absolutely still. She silently mouthed the words, AFTER FOUR - ONE TWO THREE FOUR, and the whole choir, and human podium, moved forward perfectly in step and in time with her baton. Even the candles kept in time and flickered to each swaying step the children made. All this mass movement of bodies occurred without a sound.

Barely audible at first, then increasing in volume, the soothing sound of the humming chorus from Puccini's Madam Butterfly rose from the choir to fill the huge marquee with it's sweet, haunting, wordless music. This caused many members of the audience, not all of them parents, to wipe tears from their eyes. Even the two cynical newspapermen were impressed. John must have taken twenty pictures before the whole procession had passed him by. "I'm really enjoying this," he said to Dick, "I must being losing the plot or someone has slipped a drug into my tea!" As soon as all of the children had filed onto the performance area behind the mayor the music faded away. The conductor and her dismantled human podium stood with the choir and they all took a bow together, in perfect unison, to rapturous applause.

Those that had seats then sat down as the toastmaster rang his hand bell again. "LADIEEEES AND GENTLEMEN PRAY SILENCE FOR HER WORSHIP THE MAYOR, COUNCILLOR DAPHNE MALLACOTT!"

Daphne Mallacott rose to her feet. "Well," she said, turning to the choir and smiling, "As they say in theatre land, follow that!" She paused for a moment and looked around at the faces in the huge audience. "It would be impossible for me to compete in any way with what we have just seen and heard in the last twenty minutes.."

"Thank Gawd for that!" shouted a male voice at the

74

rear of the tent. This was met with cheers and laughter from people who stood near the owner of the voice.

"..but," she continued but stopped again as the heckler was noisily ejected by the security staff, "I do have to perform two very pleasant duties this evening. First of all I hope I can speak on behalf of you all when I thank the members of Hemel Hempstead Arts and Entertainment Committee and all those volunteers who have done so much work to make this Hemel Spectacular fortnight possible. I am just about to perform the opening ceremony but immediately after that there will be a military aircraft fly-pass provided for us by the local model aircraft club. I am to tell you this is quite safe as long those of you at the front remain in your seats. So without further ado I now declare the Hemel Spectacular formally open!" She sat down to generous applause which continued as the choristers filed off the stage to be replaced by the returning brass band.

"That was nice and brief," said John.

"Not a bad speech by her standards I have to admit," said Dick, "without even one appalling gaff. Mind you the night is young. Where are you going?"

"Down to the front," said John over his shoulder, "That's where the action is going to be." He was right because in the next moment two large sections of the tent sides were lifted on each side of the marquee as the band played the Royal Air Force March. From loudspeakers around the hall came the recorded sound of jet engines as the Red Arrows, or rather miniature versions of them, flew in through the right hand gap in the tent. The nine aircraft fitted into a formation two metres across. They flew over the heads of the mayor and her guests, banked slowly and climbed to the top of the marquee leaving white trails of dry ice as the audience gasped. The gasps turned to screams in the middle of the arena as the planes dived low over the audience, completed two more circuits and finally exited through the left hand gap in the tent. The noise coming from the loudspeakers changed to the unmistakable sound of a Spitfire. The single aircraft was a perfect replica and as large as the whole of the Red Arrows' formation. It entered the tent with guns blazing, but without bullets happily, circled the inside of the marquee three times and performed a beautiful victory roll before leaving.

There was a short pause, the band stopped playing and the crowd fell silent as the lights were dimmed. A very low-pitched hum could be heard, as if from far away, then louder and louder. Several ground-based spotlights were switched on and their beams swung upwards. The band struck up the Dambusters March just as the spotlights fastened on a Lancaster Bomber near the roof of the marquee. It was flying slowly to give the impression of a full size aircraft high in the sky. Its four engines increased power and speed as it flew down to the auditorium, across the audience and out into the night. There was a ripple of applause which died away as the voice of the 'pilot' came over the loudspeakers, "OK chaps we're going in. Bomb-aimer get ready." The spotlights swung towards the entrance doorway while security staff cleared people away from the red carpet. The mayor and her guests gasped at what they could see approaching across the cricket field outside. The not so miniature Lancaster Bomber was coming closer and closer about two metres off the ground with two of it's own spotlights shining from it's underbelly.

"Take cover!" shouted the toastmaster. He wasn't quite

sure why, as he said afterwards, it just seemed to fit the occasion. The aeroplane flew into the marquee one metre above the red carpet.

"Bomb's gone!!!" shouted the 'bomb-aimer' over the loudspeakers. This was immediately evident because, as the aircraft began to climb and head for the exit, it dropped a black inflatable ball which grew larger and larger as it bounced along the carpet towards the V.I.P. table. The town's elected representatives leapt to their feet and the mayor hid behind the mace bearer. The bouncing 'bomb,'now two metres in diameter, came to a halt at the end of the red carpet just short of the mayor's party where it was swiftly captured and held stationary by four of the security staff.

The band played the Royal Air Force March again as five members of the model aircraft club, dressed as World War Two pilots complete with boots, sheepskin jackets, leather helmets and goggles marched down the red carpet waving to the audience. They shook hands with the mayor, lifted the inflatable 'bomb' onto their shoulders and carried it back the way they had come and out into the night. "You getting any good pictures?" said a voice. John recognised the Gazette editor sitting at the top table between the mayor and the chief constable.

"Yes, that's for sure. I'd have to be a pretty rotten photographer if I didn't - with all this going on."

"Great stuff. You're going to leave the camera card on my desk later aren't you?"

"Yes, of course. That won't be long actually because I'm forbidden to photograph the Great Zoldini apparently."

"Oh good! I can't stand magic acts. Would you give me a lift back to the office when you're ready? I left my car there."

"No problem … I'll meet you on the red carpet..... John was interrupted by another familiar voice speaking into a microphone near the covered skeleton.

"Good evening ladies and gentlemen. My name is Gerald Salter. I am the archaeologist in charge of the excavation of the site on Boxmoor where the highway robber James Snook was supposed to have been buried. Most of you know that the only human remains we have found so far are of a young woman. In a few minutes I shall be giving you the latest information we have on her which I'm sure you will find fascinating. But first of all I would like to call on the mayor, Councillor Daphne Mallacott, to do the unveiling."

The band started up and provided jazz music for four vocalists giving a rendering of "Dem bones dem bones, dem dry.....bones" as the mayor approached, tottering along the carpet. She clicked her fingers in time to the music in a vain attempt to get the audience to join in with no success whatsoever. Acute and caustic embarrassment filled the air. Dr.Salter looked heavenwards and Ben Carter covered his eyes with his hands. As the singers and band fell silent the mayor managed to reach the microphone which unfortunately captured a few words of her singing, "the leg bone is connected to the ankle bone..." John hurried up to Dick East who was standing across the aisle opposite Dr.Salter and the mayor. He made ready with his camera, "I don't believe this!" he whispered.

"The song was her idea apparently but just wait till she speaks. I hope you've had your anti-cringe injections."

The mayor took the microphone from Dr.Salter who then walked several metres to the side. Ben went as far as the exit and stood looking out into the night.

"I'm sorry if I have kept you waiting," she said looking

round with a wide smile. No one smiled back. "but of course it won't make any difference to this lady. She has all the time in the world. Make no bones about it! Mind you she might take a grave view of it! Let's hope that soon she will no longer be shrouded in mystery." She began to peel back the sheet, "It gives me great pleasure to unveil this, this...oesophagus. In fact I am dead pleased!" She pulled the sheet off with a flourish, handed it to the sad looking Dr. Salter and tottered back to her seat amidst sporadic applause. The band attempted to start playing "Dry Bones" again but stopped abruptly as the toastmaster touched the conductor on the elbow and shook his head.

Hardly anyone noticed Ben walking back from the exit as all eyes were on the skeleton and Dr.Salter as he returned to the microphone. His discreet smile was one of obvious relief. "Well, as I believe it was said earlier this evening by somebody.... follow that!" Most people in the crowd seemed to have erased the last few minutes and the previous speaker from their minds as they edged forward to get a good view.

"Don't worry you should all be able to see her properly in just a moment." He pressed a hand-held remote control switch to elevate his precious exhibit to head height. Then a spot light illuminated the case so it could be seen clearly from everywhere in the marquee. "Those of you who want to look more closely should be able to do so during the interval which follows immediately after I've stopped speaking," he looked at his watch, "which will be in about ten minutes." He glanced up at the skeleton and then back at the audience.

"These remains were uncovered in February this year by my friend Ben Carter who is standing next to me. Ben is one of many local volunteers who assist in me in these projects and I would like to thank him and all of his fellow unpaid workers without whom projects like this would never be undertaken. During the last two months I have had a great many requests by a multitude of people and organisations to view the skeleton - not least among them the editor and his staff at the Gazette who have shown remarkable patience when you consider how much interest there has been in this mystery."

"Hear! Hear!" said Dick East.

I want to tell you of a few issues which will help to explain why it has taken so long to go public with these remains. There are a whole list of questions to be answered. Who was she? What is she doing in Snook's coffin? When did she die? How did she die? Was she in fact the highway robber disguised as a man? This last idea is not so far-fetched as one might think. What I am going to tell you is true and historical fact. About ten miles from here is a desolate road in a place north of St. Albans called Nomansland. In 1652, many years before James Snook's time, a woman known as the Wicked Lady was shot while attempting to rob a loaded wagon on that road. She managed to ride the short distance to her home at Markyate Cell where she later died of her wounds. Her real name was Lady Katherine Ferrers who carried out many highway robberies in Hertfordshire dressed as a man.

I'm sorry to have to disappoint those amongst you who have vivid imaginations but our mystery lady is very unlikely to have been 'Miss Snook' the highway woman," he glanced at Dick East who began crossing out lines of shorthand in his notebook, "However it is still a mystery and I, like the rest of you here this evening I'm sure, would like to solve it. So if you have any theories, or better still real information, please contact me or the Gazette who will be happy to pass details on to me. I am working closely with the newspaper on this and I can promise that both the Gazette and I will respect your privacy should you want to remain anonymous.

I can now tell you the few bits of evidence that we have established. It is obvious that she was a woman because of the shape and size of her pelvis. Most of you will know that a male pelvis is quite narrow whereas a woman's is wider and the gap in the middle is wide enough for a baby's head to pass through. The pathologist confirms that she was a woman in her late twenties, in good health and, although not overweight, had eaten nutritious food all her life. She has a full set of healthy teeth which was unusual in those days. We managed to obtain the services of a specialist in facial anatomy who can build up a likeness using an exact replica of an original skull. He hasn't quite finished his work but he informs me that her face would have fitted all the conventions of normality. I think he means she would have had balanced proportions without a huge nose or manly jaw and her cheekbones are such that it would not be impossible for her to be beautiful," he raised his palms at some feminine protests from the crowd, "Please, I'm trying not to sound like I'm indulging in male fantasies. I am trying to make the point that it seems unlikely she could have been mistaken for a man- let alone have been tried and hung as highwayman. Also James Snook was known to many people and had at least one mistress in London. So if he was a woman I think someone would have noticed. When the facial anatomy specialist has finished I will be able to obtain a photograph of how she might have looked and I promise I shall let the Gazette have a copy straight away as well as putting it on the Internet. Just a few more important details. The pathologist's report says that cause of death is likely to have been from a stab wound to the chest. This is because there is definite bone damage to the front of the rib cage which could only have been caused by a sharp metal blade. He also says that there is strong evidence that she had given birth to at least one child. One last thing. Only a few piles of dust remained of whatever clothes she was wearing but we found this in her hand," Dr. Salter took a small cloth bag from his pocket and took out a silver chain with a medallion on it, "It is a St. Christopher medallion and engraved on the back are the words, 'Dearest Snook, may God carry you in his arms wherever you go. I am your love for ever, Abigail.'

Now, this isn't concrete proof but it strongly suggests that she had a connection to Snook and that her name was probably Abigail, but we don't know for certain. The remaining issue which has to be dealt with is what happens to her now. I have had very little guidance on the proper procedures or indeed whether I should have made her remains available to the public. In the end I decided to go ahead because this is obviously in the public interest. After a reasonable period of the skeleton being on view I am going to suggest that she is put back in the earth again with a proper ceremony. I am not a religious man myself but it would seem appropriate under the circumstances that she should have a Christian burial because that would have been the usual thing two hundred years ago. And of course there is the St. Christopher medallion which, if it was a gift from her, she clearly thought it worthwhile asking her God to look after Snook.

So there we are. All I would ask of everyone who comes to view the remains now and in the following weeks is that they show respect for a young woman of whom we know very little. I sincerely hope we will know a great deal more in the future." He took a step backwards to the sound of appropriately modest applause from the whole audience.

"Well done Gerry," said Ben and shook his hand. Dr.Salter switched the microphone on again.

"I have been asked to remind you that there will now be an interval of twenty minutes after which you are to be amazed by the magic of the Great Zoldini."

John noticed the editor approaching in a hurry, "Have you finished?"

John nodded, "Yes I'm done. You're in luck. I'm parked just outside by the cricket clubhouse."

"Let's go then. I've had enough of this."

On the short journey to the Gazette office John opened the conversation. "You seem happy to be getting out of there."

"Oh. It's just that I've been to hundreds of these things and I'm an unsociable old bugger anyway. As well as that I'm going on holiday tomorrow night so I want to get these pages put away as soon as I can."

"Going anywhere nice?

"Yes."

"Right," said John but thought to himself, *'sorry I asked!'*

When they arrived at the Gazette office the editor got out and took possession of John's camera card, "Would you mind hanging about at the tent just until the Great Zoldini's done his stuff. I'll pay you for your time. I know you aren't supposed to take photographs but I just want you there in case he sets fire to the place or something."

Chapter Nine

Disappearing Act

John found his space at the cricket clubhouse had been taken but managed to park at the other end of the marquee near the performance area. As he was walking round the tent he noticed a gigantic mechanical digger parked right up close to the back of the stage. As he was trying to work out out what it was doing there a huge man in a suit blocked his view. "Can I help you, sir?" asked the silhouette.

"Just being nosey," said John.

"Well you have to move on sir, this is a restricted area for health and safety reasons."

"Sure thing." He moved on as instructed but at the entrance door found his way was blocked this time by four huge men in bulging dinner jackets.

"Yes?" demanded one of them.

"I'd like to go in please."

"I'm sorry sir but you won't be able to do that. There are no photographers allowed in during the performance."

"Look. I haven't got any cameras with me so I can't take any photographs can I?"

"Well the performance is about to start so you won't be allowed in anyway."

"No it isn't. There's still five minutes to go." Darkness fell upon John as four suits towered over him blocking the light. "Okay. Okay. I didn't want to go in anyway....."

"Excuse me but this gentleman is expected. Would you let him through please." The wall of dark suits parted and John saw the welcome faces of the toastmaster and Dr. Salter. "Sorry about that," said the doctor, "They're very touchy these security chaps, especially because they saw you taking photographs earlier on. I've arranged a place for you on the gantry up with that man controlling the lighting. Best I could do I'm afraid. You should be able to see quite well from there. You haven't any cameras with you, have you?"

"I have the one on my phone- like everyone else- but I'm only here in case the tent collapses or something. By the way have you any idea why a magician would want a mechanical digger?"

"No."

"Well he's got one parked at the back of his stage." He climbed up the ladder and soon found himself in a fairly comfortable seat and although he was a long way from the stage he had a splendid view.

After an extremely loud trumpet fanfare, lightning flashes and white mist, the Great Zoldini made an impressive entrance by bursting through the paper screen on the left of the performance area. The mist faded to reveal him being carried shoulder high on to the stage by ten shapely women dressed in overalls, boots, builders' helmets and safety goggles. He leapt from them to the centre of the stage and stood with his feet apart, arms folded and glowering at the audience. He was dressed from head to toe in a bright yellow costume complete with cloak. "He looks like a cross between Batman and a daffodil," said the lighting engineer.

Then Great Zoldini began to stride to every corner of the stage explaining, very loudly and with the aid of a radio microphone, what was about to happen. He told the audience that they were to witness the most unbelievable and dangerous illusion ever performed. He advised that those people of a nervous disposition or with heart problems should leave immediately, that no scientific special effects would be used and that photography was not allowed in any form. "There are no trap doors or tunnels and it is obvious there is nothing under here but solid earth. Everything you is see this evening is really happening." He smiled for the first time as a middle-aged man in the uniform of a senior police officer walked onto the stage. "Now I would like to welcome the Chief Constable, Michael Roberts, who has kindly agreed to assist me this evening. Thank you sir. And I would also like a member of the audience to help me as well." Silence. No one moved."No? Oh well we might as well all go home then! …..... Wait a minute. Oh. Good. Thankyou madam." He walked forward with one hand outstretched towards a table with ten giggling and cheering young women. One of them, in a bright green satin dress and red shoes, was propelled onto the stage by the others.

"My God it's Susan!" said John out loud.

"Do you know her then" asked his companion.

"Yes. She's my girlfriend, but what the hell does she think she's doing?"

"Are you sure she's not a plant – you know, working for the magician."

"What? No. I don't think......" *'That's it,'* he thought to himself, *'That's her mystery job! She said she has to travel a lot- and I suppose they wouldn't want people to know about it......'*

86

On the stage Zoldini was talking again, "Would you tell me your name please?"

"Susan."

"And do you live in Hemel?"

"Yes."

"And your friends here, you're having a girls' night out?"

"It's a hen night actually."

"Are you the one getting married?"

John raised his eyebrows.

"No! It's Sylvia – in the blue dress."

John lowered his eyebrows.

"Can we have a big hand for Sylvia." Sylvia stood up briefly and waved.

"Right Susan, are you ready?"

"Yes. I think so."

One of his assistants stepped forward holding a pair of handcuffs. "Would you please examine these, Chief Constable, and make quite sure they are the genuine article."

"They seem to be in order. They were standard police issue when I was on the beat many years ago."

"Then would you please sign them with this permanent marker pen."

"Thank you. Now will you lock them on Susan and keep the key in your pocket." Meanwhile the other nine assistants approached carrying a two metre long wooden box with two holes in one end. This they placed on the floor in front of Zoldini. "Are you ready Susan?" Accepting a nod as a yes he opened the lid of the box and got her to lie down in it. He approached the end of the box which had the two holes in it and slid open the top half so she could put her feet, complete with red shoes, through the holes.

He then closed everything up and locked the lid with a padlock. The chief constable left the stage. A powerful spotlight switched on to illuminate the box. Zoldini took a hand microphone from one of his assistants and stuck it on top of the lid with gaffer tape. "Are you all right in there Susan?"

"Fine thank you!"

"Good. I'm going to leave this microphone on top of the box in case you change your mind. Can you wiggle your shoes?" The red shoes wiggled.

"Why am I doing this?"

"Just to prove you are still in there."

"Where else would I be? ….. What's that noise?" It was the distinct sound of a diesel engine starting up. Zoldini stepped back towards the large paper screen to the right of the stage while his assistants began pushing the box towards him. At the same moment a JCB mechanical digger burst through the paper screen with a tremendous noise. The assistants fell over themselves in their efforts to flee to the back of the stage. The digger sped towards the box with its steel bucket scraping along the floor. It scooped up the box and lifted it high in the air. The red shoes could be seen kicking wildly and screams rent the air. Zoldini ran forward shouting "Stop! Stop! She's still in there!" The driver didn't seem to hear him. He tipped up the bucket and the box crashed onto the floor. Then he brought the bucket down on top of the box smashing it to pieces. "Go back you fool!" shouted Zoldini climbing into the cab. As the digger reversed he jumped down and knelt beside the box which was now little more than a pile of splinters. There were screams from the hen-night revellers. The St.John Ambulance staff climbed onto the stage and the chief constable leapt to his feet. John almost threw himself from the scaffolding in his haste to reach ground level. He started running towards the stage. Zoldini was shouting "It's all right everyone she's not been hurt. She's just disappeared, but where is she?" He picked up the red shoes, which were miraculously undamaged, and walked towards the audience holding them high above his head. Several people in the crowd turned towards the entrance where a voice, Susan's voice, could be heard. "Excuse me.... Excuse me would you let me through please." John spun round as he was running, tripped, and fell into the arms of security staff. Several spotlights swung round towards the entrance. John's mouth fell open as Susan in her bright green dress, bare feet and handcuffs walked down the red carpet to the stage to a roar of applause. As she passed him she said, "Are you OK? You look ever so pale. See you tomorrow. All right?" John managed a rather useless smile and felt as if he was going to faint.

Zoldini welcomed her back onto the stage and knelt down to put her shoes back on. The chief constable unlocked the handcuffs, examined his signature and nodded his approval. Susan joined her friends who gave her multiple hugs and kisses and glasses of Champagne provided by Zoldini's assistants.

John was amazed at the kindness of the security men who sat him down on a chair and gave him a glass of water. A grinning face loomed up in front of him, "Hello mate you look as though you've seen a ghost." It was Dick East. "Here, I've got a note for you," he said handing him a scrap of paper. "The girl in the green dress said to give it to you. Have you got a thing going on with her?"

"Something like that...." he muttered.

The note said, 'Sorry about tonight. It must have scared

you a bit. I have to go off with my friends now but I want to be with you very soon. Don't be late tomorrow. I can't wait. XXXXX Susan.'

"You're a better colour now. Did you faint earlier or something?"

"Very nearly, yes." He said getting to his feet, "but I'm OK now." He could see Susan in the distance, revelling with her friends, and started to walk down the red carpet towards her but he was met by a wall of security men. "Sorry sir," said one of them, "We're clearing the tent now."

"What about those then?" asked John, pointing at large collection of people by the stage who included the mayor and her guests as well as Susan and her friends.

One of the security man, with all signs of previous kindness melted from his face, gripped John's arm firmly, "Those are the V.I.P.s and they are staying behind for a party - by invitation only."

"I've got a press ticket and a back stage pass."

"I don't care if you've got a knighthood and a machine gun you ain't going down there mate."

John found himself outside the marquee with Dick East who asked him if he wanted to go for a pint.

"Thanks Dick, but no. I'm going home now because I'm getting up early tomorrow."

Tired as he was when he got to his bedroom in Watford he was still wide awake with the after effects of his stressful evening so he busied himself with preparations for the morning. He packed a suitcase with his best casual clothes and washed and shaved. *'Of course,'* he thought to himself, *'I remember, we're going to visit Ben at his place in the afternoon,'* and with that thought and the comforting realisation that it was entirely possible he would have a blissful relaxing day with Susan he fell asleep.

Chapter Ten

Back to the Marquee

At ten past one the next morning John was dreaming. He dreamt that he was running down a moonlit road across Nomansland, chasing after a wooden box on the back of a horse and cart. The box had two holes at one end with a pair of feet poking out complete with red shoes. A woman dressed as a highwayman galloped up on a black horse and pointed her pistol at the driver of the wagon. There was a loud bang from a discharged firearm but it was she, the robber, who was shot. The driver cracked his whip and he and the horse and cart sped off into the night. The box fell onto the road and smashed to bits revealing it's contents, a human skeleton. The highway woman crouched down by the remains of the box while holding a blood-drenched hand to her shoulder. She had long straight blond hair and when she turned her head to speak he could see that it was Susan, "This is all wrong .. that was me in there but I don't wear red shoes......"

"No!" shouted John as he woke covered in sweat. He sat on the edge of the bed, took a swig from a bottle of water, held his head in his hands and asked himself, "What was that all about?" He drank some more water and headed for the shower. Minutes later he was drying himself when his mobile phone rang. "Hello..........Susan is that you? …...... No I was awake already. …... I just had this stupid dream that's all. Thank God you're OK. Are you OK?........Right … I'll come straight away. You at Herbert Street? I'll be there in less than half an hour." It took him three minutes to dress and clean his teeth. He grabbed his suitcase, car keys and mobile phone and hurried down the stairs to his car.

During the short journey along the A41 by-pass he opened the window, shook his head a few times to revive himself and shouted "I'm awake! I'm awake!" at the night sky, and then, "More than you are you silly sod!" at a fox that darted in front of his car. By the time he arrived at Herbert Street he was fully alert. He knocked on the door which was opened immediately. "Susan!" he said going up the steps with open arms, "Come here. I need you hold you right now please."Instead she stepped backwards and gestured for him to come in."What's the matter?" he asked as he dropped his suitcase in the hall and followed her into the kitchen, "Has something happened? You seem strange, different......." he stopped as she lit a cigarette, "you are different. I've never seen you smoking."

"Actually you've never seen me at all. I'm not Susan. I'm her sister."

"What?"

"We are identical twins."

"No!"

"Yes."

"I don't believe it. You. Me. We're in love..."

"No we're not. You're in love, pretty obviously, but with Susan not me. I'm Lindsey - her sister Lindsey. Look. Has she got one of these?" She removed her coat and showed him a tattoo of a scorpion on her right shoulder. "It's real, not painted on. Watch....," she caught some water from the tap and rubbed her shoulder.

"All right I believe you, I think. You are amazingly alike...... Why are you wearing Susan's clothes?" Without her coat he could see she was wearing a bright green satin dress. "Oh. I understand. You work for Zoldini as well. That's how the trick is done!"

"I'm impressed. Susan said you were intelligent."

"But where is she? And why are you here?"

"The answer to your first question is, I don't know. Secondly, the reason I'm here is because I always meet up with my sister after the performance. It's sort of re-assurance for each other, an emotional safety check. She always finishes some while after me so I came here to get a bit of supper ready for her ..... only she hasn't come. She's never missed our after-the-show get together, not once. That's why I'm worried."

"Well I don't know where she is. Wait a minute, when you called me just now why didn't you ask if she was with me? How did you know she wasn't?"

"Hey! Don't get all suspicious. I knew because when you answered you said, 'Is that you Susan?' So, because you thought I was her, I asked you to come here. I didn't want to try and explain the situation over the phone. You wouldn't have believed me anyway."

"No I wouldn't. I can hardly believe it now," He was standing opposite her. He couldn't help remembering when he stood in the kitchen looking at Susan in almost the same position less than three days before. "How worried are you? You're beginning to scare me."

"I'm scared too."

"We should call the police." John followed Lindsey

as she left the kitchen and sat down at the bottom of the stairs.

"There is a small problem with that," she said, putting her elbows on her knees and her chin in her hands, "Firstly the police have a system of not carrying out a search for twenty four hours, that is with a case like this where we have no definite reason to think she is in danger. Secondly Susan and I, and all Zoldini's employees for that matter, get paid a lot of money for what we do, which is great, but we get paid in arrears and there is a clause in the contract that if we reveal any secrets or attract any publicity we get paid nothing - zilch! So that's why I don't want the police and the press to get involved, yet. And I'm sure Susan wouldn't want it either. Have you any idea where she might be? I mean did she say anything?"

"No. I assumed she was going off with her mates."

"Those 'mates' all work for Zoldini too. There's never any 'hen night'. She usually parts with them when no one is looking and heads for home in the car. She might have looked a bit tipsy but that's part of the act. She would never drink and drive."

John took a piece of paper out of his pocket, "The only thing I have is this note from her saying she would see me tomorrow - I mean today."

Lindsey read it and looked directly at John, "Look. Can we look for her together? If we don't succeed then we'll call the police."

"All right. But when do we call them ?"

"Whenever you say. I'll go along with your instincts."

"Where do we start?"

"I think we should go back to the marquee. It could be something quite simple. She might not be able to start the car and she's probably not answering her phone because she nearly always has a flat battery. Talking of phones, I see you've got yours. I'll take mine as well. Yours will have already saved my number. I got your number from this in case you were wondering." She held one of his cards that he had given to Susan when he first met her. It seemed to John to be a long time ago. He spoke resolutely, "Right. Let's go. Now is good. I like now. We'll go in my car if you like."

"I was hoping you would say that, as Susan's got mine. Try not to worry. She's very good at looking after herself....survival skills and all that."

"I bloody hope so, he said softly." On the stairs, where Lindsey had been sitting, John could see the tea towel with 'Welcome to Hemel Hempstead' written on it.

He parked the car in the same spot he had occupied the previous evening by the cricket pavilion. It was a mild night with clouds obscuring the moon and stars but there was plenty of light coming from the lamp posts in the nearby roads to illuminate almost the whole area around the marquee. Several caravans formed a half circle, wagon train style, around the rear of the marquee. Most had lights behind their little net curtains and many were flickering with the tell-tale glimmer of television screens. "Any idea who these people are? They might know something. Are they part of your stage crew?" asked John as they got out of the car. He took a large torch from the boot and they set off towards the marquee.

"No. I don't know who they are - maybe the people who put up the tent. Our lot would have been home in bed ages ago and you can never get in touch with Zoldini. He wouldn't care anyway." They were walking past the marquee across the cricket field towards a car parked by the canal. "There, that's my car... ...That's odd, the driver's door is open..... The keys aren't there. She must have taken them with her."

John was looking at the front of the car, "Come and have a look at this." The ground was very soggy and both wheels had sunk into deep groves in the turf. Mud was also splattered along the sides and the doors as if the wheels had spun while someone made a frantic effort to drive away. "She must have got stuck, obviously, and walked off to get some help."

"Because my sister's phone has no battery again, probably. There it is on the back seat. I'm right. It's dead as a door nail. But where would she have gone?" She put the phone in her coat pocket.

The only other vehicle nearby was a huge four-wheel-drive estate car parked further along the bank of the canal. As they approached it John shone the torch on the windows. It was full of sleeping young men packed in like sardines. Tapping on the windows produced no reaction from those inside apart from a youth in the driving seat who opened one eye, poked his middle finger in the air and went to sleep again. John was just about to increase the force of his window-tapping when Lindsey called out from where she stood on the edge of the canal. "Hey," she said, " Bring your torch over here. What you make of these?"

Chapter Eleven

Nell Gwyn

A few hours before, at around eleven in the evening, Susan and her 'hen night' pals were almost the last to leave the marquee. They were in a good mood and hardly had to act their parts as they pushed and shoved each other and giggled their way to their cars parked by the canal. They hugged the 'bride to be', wished her 'good luck on Saturday', said their farewells and drove off into the night - all except for Susan. She sat in Lindsey's car and tried to phone John's mobile without success. "No frigging battery again!" she said to herself throwing the now useless instrument onto the back seat. *'Oh well, let's head for home'* she thought, as she put her key in the ignition, *'Never mind I'll see him tomorrow,....him and his cute ....'* There was a tap on her driver's side window and a face so close it was almost touching the glass.

"JESUS CHRIST!! You scared me half to death." It was a woman's face, wearing a white linen cap, a cloak and a friendly smile so she opened the window. "You made me jump!"

"Sorr-ee. Didn't mean to. I wonder if you can help me. I'm a bit lost. I'm looking for Brian Smith. No that's not right, I can't see..." she said, trying to read from a crumpled piece of paper.

Susan opened the passenger door, "Get in. You'll be able to read it in here."

"Thanks ever so much. That's better. No look, it's not Smith it's Smythe, Brian Smythe. Do you know him?"

"No."

"Sorry. I just thought I'd ask. I don't know what else to do. I'm supposed to meet him 'ere by the canal. Him and his friends are having a stag night on a barge called Nancy. I fink that's it there- you can just see it, only the name's all faded and there's no one there."

Susan peered through the darkness in the direction her companion was pointing. She could just make out the barge and the dark silhouette of huge man, also in a cloak, standing by it, "Who's that."

"Oh, it is all right. That's my boyfriend. My name's Ellie Green. Ellie is short for Eleanor. At school they called me Nell - Nell Green and that ended up as Nell Gwyn. So when I started my own business I stuck with the name. Look, have some of me cards - give them to your friends." She gave Susan a whole packet of visiting cards which bore the message,

"Gorillagrams, Nun-o-grams, a policewoman,
a fireman, or why not have the best-
a
NELL GWYN -O-GRAM!"

Beneath this was printed a mobile telephone number.

"That's me," she said proudly, "This lot asked for Nell Gwyn and they're goin' to get her. This is my outfit. I've got all the assets - as well as the oranges if you know what

I mean!" She giggled like a machine gun. "Would you like an orange......er....what's your name luv?"

"Susan."

"Go on have one, I've got plenty.

"Thank you," said Susan, taking the orange and the cards, "but you will have to excuse me. I'm tired and I have to drive home now. I'm sorry I don't know where your friends are."

"They're not friends. Good job an' all. Snotty load of stuck-up upper class dick-heads if they're anything like this Smythe bloke. I've a good mind to go home. It makes no odds to me. I've got me money. Everyone has to pay up front." She got out of the car, and shouted across to her boyfriend, "What d'yer reckon, we've been here twenty minutes. Shall we leave it?"

"Yeah."

"He don't say much but he's a lovely man. Bye-ee!"

Susan tried to see what her 'lovely man' looked like but all she had was a rear view of them both as they walked off arm-in-arm across the now deserted field - he carrying her basket of oranges and she with her ample posterior and ample everything else.

'Look at the time!' thought Susan, *'Lindsey will be wondering where I am... with my supper all ready too. I'm so hungry but I'll be there in five minutes.'* She started the car, attempted to drive away and the wheels promptly sank into the soft mud. She tried second gear, third gear, reversing. With lack of care born out of tiredness and frustration she was doing these manoeuvres without a safety belt which resulted in her being thrown forward. The top of the steering wheel collided with her neck and whacked into her windpipe. "Ouch that really hurt!" she tried to say but could only manage a whisper. *'My bloody*

voice has gone,' she thought, *'now what am I going to do?'* She ripped open the orange and sucked the juice to try to relieve her throat. She tried to speak but still no sound came, *'I'll have to walk to the road and hope a taxi comes by, or walk home..........'*

A huge four-wheel-drive estate car with massive tyres came bouncing across the field and came to a violent halt by the canal a few metres in front of her. Nine prosperous looking young men piled noisily out of the doors carrying bottles and glasses. *'That thing could give me a tow,'* she thought, *'anyway there's enough of them to push me out easily.'* She peered through the gloom and could just see them carrying, with great hilarity, one of their companions horizontally on their shoulders from the estate car across the grass and into the barge. Her throat was less painful now but could still only manage a squeaky whisper, *"I'll have to do sign language and keep pointing at the car,"* she thought. She began looking around for some writing materials. She found a pen in the glove compartment but nothing to write on but the packet of Nell Gwyn's visiting cards. She wrote 'PLEASE GIVE MY CAR A PUSH' on one of them, put the other cards and her keys into her handbag and went to meet them. She waved to get their attention. "Hello," she mouthed silently, pointing at her tonsils, "I've lost my voice."

"She's arrived, gentlemen. Welcome fair maiden," said a young man in a crumpled dinner jacket and a bow tie hanging down his chest. He seemed to be their leader, "I'm sorry we're late. Thank you for waiting," He swayed slightly and so did his companions who quickly surrounded her. They were holding various bottles and glasses and stared at her with obvious delight. The young man spoke again slurring his speech and staggering a

100

little, "My name is Brian Smythe shomething-or-other, never mind that. I'm the one who called you and sent you the money. You're Nell Gwyn of course."

Susan shook her head and mouthed, "No, I'm not. I'm just want your help." He didn't seem to understand, or couldn't be bothered, so she handed him the card with her message written on it.

He took the card from her but only looked at the printed side and threw it on the ground, "That's right...I know... Nell Gwyn. We're all ready for you." Susan shook her head again, turned back towards the car and was immediately overtaken by the mob of young men who carried her off to the barge. They stood her on her feet by the gangplank and grouped round her in a tight circle. She glared at them defiantly, red faced and panting.

"I like the green dress," said one of her captors, "but you don't look much like Nell Gwyn to me - and where are your oranges?"

"Absolutely gorgeous," said another upper class voice.

"Bloody marvellous piece of totty," said another, "very fit for purpose."

"Yes," said Brian Smythe, "I'm sorry you've lost your voice. Have a little drinkie, how about some Champagne?" Susan shook her head, "No? Ah well you don't need your voice for what we want you to do." His companions began to snigger. Susan froze with terror. This must have shown in her face because their leader spoke again, "Oh. Don't worry, not with us, with Giles, our man in the boat, the groom. He's getting married next Saturday and this is probably his last chance of freedom and happiness. So this is where you come in, you provide him with enough happiness and we'll pay you double. All aboard who's coming aboard!" he shouted as they all climbed onto the barge and dragged Susan with them. They opened the door to the cabin at the rear of the boat, pushed her inside, and turned the key in the lock.

There was just enough light to make out her surroundings. The space contained two bunk beds. One of these was occupied by another young man who was asleep, or in a drunken stupor. He, or his companions, had removed his shoes and spread his dinner jacket over him as a blanket. On the other bunk was a pile of unopened cans of lager. She looked around the cabin for a means of escape. There was a porthole on either side and each was covered with a small curtain. She drew one aside, saw grinning faces staring at her and hastily put it back again. The porthole on the opposite wall faced dry land with no sign of anybody but this, like the one on the other side, was too narrow to escape through. Her fear had largely subsided now but what remained was anger and determination. She was thinking clearly and rapidly. '*What do I do now?*' she asked herself. She looked at her unwanted companion, '*I'm not scared of him, he's another waste of space. I'm sorry for the bride, though. Who'd want to marry him - or any of his useless friends for that matter - however much money they've got.*' She looked towards the porthole again, '*Lindsey! She's bound to come looking for me - only I've got her car. She'll probably get a taxi. I know she won't call the police - not for a while anyway.*' She opened her handbag, '*I suppose I could write a message on something. Hell! I haven't even got a lipstick. I could have written on the glass with that. What about Nell Gwyn's cards. I can write on those. Oh no. I haven't brought the bloody pen!*'

She heard the boat's engine starting up and amidst all the shouting and laughing outside she could hear Brian Smythe giving orders,

"Let's get under way. Cast off fore and aft!" Susan could feel the barge moving and then saw grass and weeds passing by outside. *'I'd better do something quick!'* she thought. She opened the porthole and threw handfuls of Nell Gwyn's cards onto the canal bank.

Chapter Twelve

The Stag Party

John strode quickly towards Lindsey and shone his torch on the ground where she was pointing. "They're visiting cards," she said, "about twenty of them, all over the place and along the edge of the canal and some of them floating on the water."

John crouched down for a closer look, "It seems at first that they've been scattered just anywhere but close to the water there is a pattern .. three here.... and three there."

"Threes!," they both said together, then John,

"It's Susan! It's her survival techniques." They hastily gathered them up and examined them by the light of the torch, "They're all the same..... There's a mobile number. Let's call this Nell Gwyn and see if she knows anything." As she was dialling the number John was looking at the backs of the cards and found the one with the message, 'PLEASE GIVE MY CAR A PUSH'. He showed it to Lindsey, "That's my sister's writing …Hello. Is that Nell Gwyn?" She tilted her phone so John could hear the other side of the conversation.

"No it's not," it was a man's voice, "Do you know what time it is?"

"Yes I do. I'm really sorry but I promise you this is an emergency. Could I please speak to her? Tell her it's regarding my sister Susan, I'm hoping she might know her - or even better where she is...." Silence........... "Please don't hang up,"..... the agonising silence continued..........

"Hello. I'm Ellie Green. Who's that?"

"I'm Lindsey. I'm looking for my sister Susan who has gone missing. We found some of your cards by the canal - not far from my sister's car. We're down here now having a look round. I was hoping you might know where she is."

"No. Dunno. I'm sorry. I can't help you."

"No. Don't hang up please. Do you know how your cards got there?"

"Oh. I remember now. Susan, yes. The last time I saw her she was in her car and I asked her to help me find someone. That's it - and I gave her an orange. I gave her a box of me cards too."

"Do you mind if I ask who you were looking for?"

"It was a posh sounding bloke, said his name was Brian Smythe. He wanted me to come as Nell Gwyn to his friend's stag party on a barge called Nancy - only there was no one there and I got fed up of waiting. Is that any help? I'll call you if I fink of anyfink else"

"Yes, thank you. Good bye."

"Good bye, 'ope you find her soon." Lindsey put the phone in her pocket and looked at John.

"We'll have to wake up those blokes in the estate car. I bet they know something." As they approached they could see some of the occupants standing with their backs to them and urinating on the grass. John turned to Lindsey and whispered, "I think I know how to deal with this. If you trust me go and sit in your car, record everything on your phone and come out when I shine my torch at you."

Lindsey nodded and silently hurried across the grass. The driver's door was still open so she was able to hide herself without making a sound. John waited till they had all finished their calls of nature and said "Hello" loudly and coldly. They all turned towards him at the same time. "Who the devil are you?" asked one of them.

"Never mind who I am. Is Brian Smythe here because if he is I would like to speak to him."

"You're speaking to him," said Brian Smythe stepping down from a side door of the estate car. He leant one shoulder against the vehicle and lit a cigarette. "What can I do for you?" John could see that he was drunk and, by observing the size of his pupils, was fairly certain that he had taken drugs as well. As it was obvious this man had no intention of moving from where he stood John walked towards him instead, "I'm looking for Susan Savage and I rather think you know where she is."

"Do you now," said Smythe looking at John behind half closed eyelids, "Why do you think that, you dreadful oick, and where did you get my name from?"

"From somebody who calls herself Nell Gwyn. You paid her to come to your little party this evening - only she went home because she couldn't find you."

A glimmer of understanding showed for a moment behind the drugged and inebriated eyes. They were now surrounded by the rest of his companions.

"Well I don't know any Nell Gwyn or any tart called Susan Savage for that matter. So go away."

"I don't think so."

"This says so." Smythe reached inside the car, brought out a double barrelled shot gun and pointed it at John's face.

"No it doesn't, for several reasons. One, you haven't

got the gall to shoot anybody. Two, the noise of a gun going off would bring all those people out of their caravans and all your little chums here would pee their pants with fright and, lastly, my friend sitting in the car over there has been recording everything that's been happening on her mobile phone and relaying the whole thing to my internet site. So put it away you silly little man." John felt himself sweating with fear but he managed to flash his torch towards Lindsey who promptly got out of the car and walked across the grass towards them taking photographs of the scene with her phone as she approached. This caused a sensation because of her similarity to Susan and also because she was wearing an identical dress.

"How did she get out?" exclaimed Smythe, "and what's happened to Giles?" John wrenched the gun from him and placed it across his neck, clamping him against the door. He spoke through gritted teeth, "So, are you still saying you don't know anything you little prick? Where is she?" Smythe pointed at Lindsey, "No that's not her, that's her sister." He released some pressure on his victim's neck so he could speak, "WHERE IS SHE?"

A red headed youth spoke up "She's with Giles in a barge called Nancy...."

"Don't tell him Ginger," said Smythe.

"Listen Ginger," said John, loud enough for everyone to hear, "you are all in a lot of trouble. Just think how much evidence there is so far. We have photographs of you all, some showing this idiot holding a gun, and recordings of the conversation.

I strongly suggest you tell me where this barge is."

Ginger pointed, "Down the canal, that way, in the first lock you come to."

John increased the pressure on Smythe's neck who began to turn blue. "Give me the keys to this car," he demanded. Smythe handed them over and promptly collapsed to the floor. John turned towards the other young men who were beginning to look like a herd of sheep. "Why is she in the barge and who is Giles?"

"Giles is the one who is getting married next Saturday," said Ginger, "We locked him in a cabin with Nell Gwyn. That's who we thought she was, honestly. It was only a bit of fun."

"Fun?," snarled John, looking directly at all their faces, "If this is what you call fun I'd hate to see what you call malicious." He took the cartridges out of the gun and threw them into the canal. "Now get out of the way." He held the gun by the barrels and swung it in front of him, scything his way through the youths.

"What's going to happen now?" asked Ginger.

"I haven't decided yet. Think about it till I get back." Lindsey held John's hand for a moment as they hurried along the canal bank towards the lock. "Well done," she said, "You're not a drip are you?"

"Thank you," said John quickening his pace, "but we'd better get a move on."

"I'm sure she'll be all right. I think it's more likely we'll have to rescue this Giles person before she kills him!"

"Oh my God! Look at that!" said John as they caught site of the lock. The barge was now tilted at such an angle it looked like the last few minutes of the sinking of the Titanic. They both began running as fast as they could.

Chapter Thirteen

Broken Gun

After a short time the engine slowed and Susan could see that they were passing through some lock gates. Then the engine stopped and so did the barge. Above her the shouting and laughing had stopped to be replaced by whispers and the occasional "Shhh!"

Someone said, "Let's see how they're getting on," and the cabin door was unlocked and opened to reveal a collection of ogling faces. Susan flung one of the cans at them which burst on the door frame covering them in lager. She immediately threw another which hit one of them full in the face. They withdrew and locked the door again. Susan could hear Smythe's voice again, "Let's leave them to it."

"We can wait in the car," said another.

"Suppose he just sleeps all night?" said someone else.

Brian Smythe again, "I know what will wake him up. Untie that mooring rope. Yes that one," then, after a pause, "Right, everyone off the boat." Susan could feel the barge rocking as nine people jumped ashore then, after, "This ought to do the trick," she could hear the rattle of a ratchet wheel and then the sound of rushing water. The voices and laughter receded as her captors walked away. *'What the hell have they done now?'* she asked herself. She began to realise what they had done when the barge began descending like a lift, *'They've opened the sluice to drain the lock- but why?'* Then, as the cabin began to tilt enough for loose objects to slide along the floor, she realised why, *'The bastards have left it tied up at one end!'* These events seemed have the desired effect on the future groom because he woke up to find himself sliding feet first towards the lower end of his bunk. "I say. This is a bit off. What the devil's happening?" Susan decided to ignore him. She began climbing up towards the cabin door which, because of how much the barge was tilting, was now more in the position of a loft trap door than an entrance way.

"Where's all this blasted H2O coming from?" asked her companion. Muddy liquid was bubbling up through the floor and was now level with his knees. He made a vain attempt to catch his shoes as they floated away from him. The water outside was now lapping against the port hole. Susan managed to climb up and lay on her back on the end of one of the bunks. From there she was able to lift her legs up and press her feet against the door. She pressed as hard as she could but this had no effect whatsoever. She began kicking wildly in a spasm very close to panic. She stopped because she could hear a voice, "That you Susan? Keep calm luv, I'll 'ave you aht in a jiffy."

'I know that voice,' she thought. There was a crunching sound and the door was lifted open. Susan was blinded by the light of a torch until it was put to one side, then she saw the grinning face of her rescuer.

"Ello luv. Remember me?"

Susan almost fell off into the water, "My God! It's

Craig!" She was looking directly at the face she last saw on the floor of The Old Bell public house with a dessert spoon up his nostril. Another face appeared alongside the first, that of Ellie Green, this time without her Nell Gwyn costume, "Ello again Susan. This is my boyfriend Craig. You've met before, I fink."

Susan looked from one to the other with her mouth open and wild-eyed with astonishment, "Yes," she said hoarsely, but much relieved that she could speak again.

Ellie was speaking again at high speed as usual, "Craig almost recognised you when I was sitting in your car but when he heard me say 'Susan' he remembered who you were an' insisted that we came down 'ere to 'elp look for you. He 'eard me talking about you on the phone when your sister called me."

"My sister?"

"Yes," said Ellie, "She phoned me when she found me visiting cards. You must have dropped 'em somewhere. I told her about the stag party and the boat. It's all right. Craig is a changed man and doesn't drink any more. And about that time - you know - when you met before - well 'e wants to apologise, don't yer Craig."

"Yeah. No 'ard feelings, eh luv?" he said and held out his hand.

"None at all," said Susan sweetly, "But if it's not too much trouble would you mind lifting me out of here? I think my feet are going to get wet very soon."

"He's a lovely man really."

As the three of them stepped onto dry land Ellie said, "Your sister must be here somewhere and it sounded like there was someone with her."

"And there she is!" said Susan, "and that's *my* 'lovely man' with her." She ran towards them - only a few paces because John was arriving fast. To avoid a collision he took her into his arms and swung her round in a circle- only once because they were overwhelmed with an immediate need to cover each other with kisses.

"Aaaah!" said Ellie, "innit luvly Craig?"

"Yuss," said Craig.

Lindsey, who had been standing with her weight on one leg and her arms folded, grinned and said, "Hello Sis." Susan relaxed her hold on her lover and hugged her sister.

"I knew you would come. Thank you. Thank you. ..... Why are you holding a shot gun?"

"It belongs to that Smythe idiot. John took it off him."

"Did he?"

"Oh yes. He's quite a hero your boyfriend."

"I know," she put her arm round him again and Lindsey hugged them both, "but you can't have him, he's mine!" Reluctantly she broke away from their loving embraces as she remembered her manners,"Introductions. John and Lindsey, these two are real heroes as well. They rescued me from the boat. This is Ellie and her boyfriend Craig."

Ellie shook hands with Lindsey, "We spoke on the phone but it's really nice to meet you."

John shook hands with Craig. Susan saw the bewildered expression on her lover's face and said,

"Yes. You have met before, in the Old Bell pub... Craig is a changed man apparently. We've agreed to forget that incident. It never happened. Isn't that right Craig?"

"Yuss."

Ellie was looking slightly puzzled, "Why have you got the same dresses on?"

Lindsey answered her, "It's a bit of a long and complicated story..........What's that?" She stopped and everyone turned towards the barge.

"Would somebody help me please," said a pitiful voice, "I can't get out and I'm soaking wet."

"Oh, that's Giles," explained Susan, "He's the one the party's for but I don't think he's enjoying it much!"

A few minutes later four tired but happy people, and one miserable wet one, walked side by side towards the sad and deflated young men who stood by the estate car. Ginger came to meet them, glancing towards Craig as John gave him the shotgun to hold, "I'm glad you're back safely - all of you that is...." He stopped because they all walked straight past him as if he wasn't there. "Are you all right Giles?"

"No," said Giles.

"I think you ought to give him some of your dry clothes or a blanket or something," said John without looking at anyone in particular, "but I have to admit I don't really care a toss what any of you do. Susan, it looks as though some little magic elves have pushed your sister's car out of the mud." Ginger and the others looked for a slight sign of gratitude but none was forthcoming.

"God, I hope I've still got the keys," said Susan, rummaging in her handbag, "Yes, here they are," then to John she said, "I want to go home now."

"Go on. You go. Are you all right to drive?"

"I'm fine. Are you coming Lindsey?"

"Yes, but I'll drive you. It is my car after all, underneath all that mud. We'll be home in five minutes and I'll warm up your supper in two shakes. It's only soup."

"Soup will be heaven- if I can keep awake that is. Goodbye Ellie and Craig and thanks again. Will you be all right on your own John? …. Why are you looking at me like that."

"Oh, nothing. I'll tell you later," he said, smiling.

"I'll stay for a bit if you like," said Craig.

"Thanks," said John.

"He's a lovely man," said Ellie, "I'll stay too."

After the two sisters had driven off there was a strange silence. Ginger spoke first, "What happens now?"

"I'll tell you in a minute. First of all where is Brian Smythe?"

"He's asleep, more like unconscious actually. I could try to wake him up but I really don't think there's any point."

"Craig, pass me the gun please." There were a few anxious faces as he walked towards the estate car. "This gun is very expensive, beautiful craftsmanship, must be worth a few thousand quid. The trouble is I get really angry when someone points a gun at me." The estate car had a front bumper like a steel girder. John pushed the barrels of the gun behind it, "Can you give me a hand," he said to Craig. They both took hold of the butt and heaved until the barrels were bent at an angle of ninety degrees. Then they turned the gun around and wedged the stock behind the bumper. With one twist they reduced the butt and trigger mechanism to splinters of wood and bits of metal. John handed the pieces to Ginger, "Please give this to him with my compliments when he wakes up," he said, then after a short pause he spoke to the rest of the deflated party goers, "The only reason I haven't got the police involved so far is because Susan and her sister don't want to attract any publicity. You should consider yourselves very lucky. I have enough evidence to convict you all on charges of assault, abduction, unlawful imprisonment, and various acts of threatened violence including the use of a firearm. This evidence I intend to put in a sealed envelope and give to my solicitor. I hope I never see or hear from any of you ever again. Now, the only thing that remains is the wrecked barge in the lock. Where did it come from?"

"Brian hired it," said Ginger, "I know he had to pay a huge deposit on it so that should cover cost of the damages. He has plenty of money."

John held up keys to the estate car, "Can one of you drive? I mean are you sober enough? Actually I don't really give a damn what you do or what happens to you. I'm too bloody tired." He threw the keys on the grass, turned his back on them said goodbye to Ellie and Craig and walked to his own car.

He arrived at Herbert Street five minutes later, remembered he still had the key to the back door and let himself in. As he suspected there was no signs of anyone being awake. He found his suitcase in the hall where he left it and carried it upstairs. The door of Susan's room was open and in it he discovered the two sisters sound asleep on top of the duvet still wearing identical green dresses. They were both lying on their right shoulders so no tattoo was visible. He had no notion which of them was Susan. "This is getting more and more bizarre," he thought. He carried his suitcase into the other bedroom and, like everyone else in the house, collapsed on the bed fully clothed and slept soundly.

Chapter Fourteen

Peace at last

After a deep dreamless sleep John woke up at ten o'clock with sunlight streaming through the window. He threw off his clothes, placed them in a pile by the bed and headed for the shower. Like most showers this one had two settings, eeeee! and ooooo! - the first being too cold and the other close to scalding. With decreasing levels of suffering he managed to find a happy medium. However he soon found his bliss interrupted with spasmodic sharp temperature drops at the eeeee! level and concluded that the shower in the other room was being used at the same time. His responding attempts to keep the temperature steady by rapid adjustments must have had adverse effects on the plumbing because he could hear multiple shrieks and giggles coming from the other room. Finally the occupants of both showers enjoyed their rediscovered aquatic bliss for a good five minutes. John tried very hard not to imagine what was going on the next room. He failed.

On his way out of the shower he needed to pull on his jeans in haste following a knock on the door, "Come in-whoever you are!"

"Good morning!" said the twins simultaneously as they burst in. They were drying their hair with towels which were in addition to the white bath towels they had wrapped themselves in. They dipped their bare right shoulders at him to show who had the tattoo. "We're now going to make a solemn promise to you," said Susan.

Then they both spoke together again, "We, Susan and Lindsey Savage, solemnly swear never to play tricks on Mr. Street and always make it obvious to him which one of us is which." They made a gesture which involved them both putting one foot and one hand out towards him, "Ta-rah!"

"Thank you. You don't know how pleased I am to hear you say that. One more favour please, could you stop talking at the same time - or sort of limit it a bit. Sorry, it's very charming but a bit scary."

The sisters glanced at each other then Susan said, on her own, "OK, done. Do you want some breakfast?"

"Yes please. I'm starving."

"Shredded Wheat and scrambled eggs?" John and Lindsey nodded enthusiastically, "Be down in ten minutes then. Oh, can you bring your clothes and things into my room because Lindsey's stuff's in here and she wants to get ready so she can go home straight after breakfast."

John, left alone with Lindsey, crammed all his things into his suitcase and paused in the doorway, "I'm so glad to have met you, bizarre as it was, and thanks for phoning me last night."

"Nice to meet you too. I thought we made a good team."

"Street and Savage, trouble shooters - very professional."

"Don't you mean Savage and Street?"

"Of course. When will we see you again and where do you live?"

"I live in Barnet, north London, and you'll see me very soon - Thursday evening, here, for dinner."

"I don't know anything about this."

"Don't worry. Susan only thought of it this morning. If you can't make it she said she will arrange it for another night. It'll just be us three and Ben Carter. She hasn't said anything to him yet either. She was going to ask him this afternoon."

"Of course! We're going to his place today. I'd almost forgotten."

"You're going there at three o'clock. You see I know every detail of your life, past present and future! Now excuse me I have to get ready."

John got dressed rapidly, or rather put his jumper and shoes on. He caught the smell of coffee drifting up the stairs and for a moment breakfast became the most important thing in the world. Then he heard the rumble of a gong followed by Susan calling up the stairs and being silly, "If you please, milady, milord, breakfast his bein' served hat this very moment."

John was standing by the breakfast table before the gong stopped resonating, "By 'eck I'm famished. Where's me grub, lass?" Susan didn't answer but kissed him instead while he held her close, "I'm so happy," she said at last.

"Me too."

"Sit down. Do you want a grapefruit juice?"

"Thank you. Oh, and I'm OK for dinner on Thursday. Lindsey just told me."

"Oh good. I promise I won't keep you waiting in desperate hunger for hours. Can't have you walking out on me!"

"How do you keep your towel from falling off?"

"It's not just a towel, it's a 'Towel Tube.' Lindsey made it. They're much better that bath robes," she did a twirl, "See, it's a tube. There's no zip or anything. It's made of soft towelling but it elasticated, that's how it stays on. It feels really nice to wear, really soft on the skin. People like them for the beach especially. She sells lots of them, in her shop."

"Lindsey has a shop?"

"Yes. She makes all the clothes herself, mostly dresses like this towel thing. The shop's called "Tubes are Us." She owns the building in Barnet High Street and lives in the flat above. She really enjoys creating stuff and is not too bothered about making lots of money. Her real job is being a stunt woman for films, and, like me, the occasional magical stuff."

"I was going to ask you, are you worried about the professional secrets bit? Loads of people must have recognised you last night. The Gazette will be interested too."

"I'm not bothered. It's happened before in other towns and with other newspapers. I just tell them I have lots of personal issues and don't want to speak to anybody. They usually leave me alone then. It would only be a problem if they found out about Lindsey or how the trick worked," She put a strangle hold on John, "and of course you're not going to tell them are you, darling ?"

"The thought never crossed my mind - and I don't know how it was done anyway."

"Well just to prove that we trust you I think you should be told. What do you think, Lindsey?" she asked her sister as she entered the room, "shall we tell him?"

"Yes tell him. He knows half of it already."

"OK, I'll start," said Susan pouring her sister a grapefruit juice, "First of all have you worked out which of us went in the box?"

"Well, I had no idea at the time because I thought it was just you but, yes, you spoke to me as you came into the marquee so Lindsey must have been in the box?"

"Yes. She painted over her tattoo and spent the early evening with her 'hen night friends'. She pretended to get a bit tipsy and then 'reluctantly agreed' to go onto the stage with Zoldini where the police chief signed the handcuffs with a marker pen, put them on Lindsey and kept the key."

Lindsey spoke next, "You may have noticed that the box was quite big. You probably didn't notice how many assistants were on the stage in their overalls and helmets. Well there were ten and it's quite a strong clue when I tell you that at the end of the performance there were eleven. One of them was me. The box was large because it contained a set of overalls, helmet, goggles, boots, a small black bag, some machinery, a small voice recorder with an amplifier and a key for the handcuffs. I had to work very fast during the three minutes that Zoldini locked up the box and continued with his patter. You might think it's bit difficult using a key to unlock handcuffs when your hands are behind you but it only takes a few seconds and there were spare keys taped to the inside of the box. Then I took off the red shoes and put them on a pair of inflatable feet. These I pushed out of the end of the box and Zoldini fixed them in the two holes. These false feet were attached to a little machine which made them wiggle now and again. The machine was radio controlled by a man at the side of the stage. This man also controlled the voice recorder and amplifier so that it seemed that I was having a conversation with Zoldini. We rehearsed this many, many times and at one stage we did try using my real voice but we realised it was too dangerous with all the things I had to do in such a short time. The amplifier was much better because it meant that my 'voice' could be heard right up to the moment when the digger lifted up the box with me 'screaming'.

I had two minutes to put the overalls on over my dress, pull on the boots, put on the helmet and goggles and last of all put the handcuffs into the black bag . The side of the box that was facing away from the audience was hinged on the top edge and held in place at the bottom with a small piece of masking tape. As soon as I was ready I kicked the side open and rolled out of the back of the box keeping flat on the floor so I couldn't be seen by the audience. This was the signal for the digger to start up. It crashed through the paper screen making a very powerful distraction for the audience. This is when I joined the gang of assistants as they scrambled to the back of the stage. A couple of them deliberately fell over behind the box so, in the very unlikely case that anyone was looking at them instead of the digger, no one would have noticed me getting up off the floor with the others. Also I was in comparative darkness because of the spotlights on the digger and the front of the box. As you saw, the digger picked up the box, complete with my 'screams', and smashed it onto the ground. When the digger bucket crashed down on the box the inflatable feet burst and the shoes fell onto the ground undamaged. The bucket destroyed all the mechanical bits inside as well as the amplifier. So, all I had to do was stand at the back of the stage and pass the black bag through a gap in the tent to a waiting 'security man'. He ran round outside the entrance to the marquee where Susan was waiting in her hiding place, behind a door marked 'Staff Only', in her green dress and no shoes."

"You finish your breakfast sis," interrupted Susan, "Well, as you might have gathered, I had the easy part. The security man put the handcuffs on me and all I had to do was walk in the entrance, looking slightly dazed and confused, and accept all the glory and applause - for doing nothing at all really. It's a weird way to earn money I must admit."

John was looking thoughtful, "And the police chief checked his signature on the handcuffs so even if people guessed you had a twin they would have a job explaining that bit."

"Zoldini might be weird," said Susan, "but he and his team are very clever at what they do."

"Isn't it dangerous for you though?" John asked Lindsey.

"Not really. Nothing was allowed to happen until I was well clear of the box."

"I bet you had to keep on good terms with the back stage man and the digger driver."

"Oh yes, you just have to trust some people. Anyway, to finish up, one of the security men whisked me off in a car so there was no chance of us both being seen at the same time. He dropped me off here and later on I called you when I started to get worried." She stood up, "Listen, I have to go. I have to meet a buyer at the shop this afternoon."

"Are you going to be late?" asked Susan.

Lindsey looked at her watch, "Actually I've got plenty of time but I want to get everything ready before he arrives."

"Business on a Sunday?" said John.

"Oh yes. He's Jewish and super rich and very high up in the rag trade. If he wants a meeting on a Sunday - he gets a meeting on a Sunday."

"Lindsey's wearing another one of her works of art," said Susan to John, "Show him sis."

Lindsey performed a few quick poses showing off a very similar garment to Susan's towel dress only it was tan-coloured and covered in fringes from top to bottom, "This is my latest creation," she said, "Do you think it makes me look like a 1920's 'flapper'--- about to do the Charleston?" She noted their nods of approval, grabbed the handle of her bag on wheels and headed for the door.

Susan kissed her as she left, "Thanks for the rescue, sis."

"Any time. No....... not any time. Never again, please. You keep her out of trouble, John ---- Bye."

Susan went back into the kitchen and closed the door by leaning her back against it with her hands behind her. The door clicked shut. They looked at each other across the kitchen. John spoke first, "We're going to Ben's place at three o'clock. It's half eleven now, what would you like to do till then?" he asked as he walked towards her. When they were face to face Susan whispered, "You could find out how I get out of a Tube Towel."

They scrambled up the stairs to Susan's room and locked the door.

Down below Lindsey stood on the doorstep looking at her car. The mud splatters acquired the night before had dried and a casual observer might have thought that it had been used for rallying. A far from casual observer in the form of a policewoman was looking at it and writing in a notebook. "Is this your car, madam?" she asked.

"Yes," said Lindsey, "is there a problem?"

"Would you mind if I came in for a few minutes? I need to ask you a some questions."

"Well, this isn't my house. My sister lives here but I don't think she will mind." she opened the door with her key, "Come through, she's in the kitchen - no she's not.... must still be asleep." She lowered her voice, "Never mind. This won't take long will it?" She closed the door after the policewoman had sat down at the table.

"I'm WPC Foster and you're Lindsey Savage,is that right?"

"Yes."

"Were you in your car near the marquee in Boxmoor late last night?"

"Yes."

"Did you have any problems? The reason why I'm asking is that we received reports of an incident soon after midnight. A few residents of St. John's Road reported some kind of confrontation between the occupants of two vehicles, one of them with your registration number and another larger vehicle-but we don't have a number for that one."

Barely audible sounds could be heard coming from the floor above. WPC Foster glanced up at the ceiling but Lindsey gazed straight ahead. "Well, my car got stuck in some muddy ground by the canal and a bunch of lads arrived and pushed it out for me. They were on a stag night I think," she said, more or less truthfully.

"One of the residents told us she thought she saw someone carrying a gun of some sort."

Lindsey stared at the notebook so that she could lie more efficiently, "I don't know anything about a gun. I didn't see anything like that when I was there. I couldn't say what happened after I went home though." The truth of the last sentence allowed her to look the policewoman in the eye again.

The lampshade above the kitchen table began to wobble and more recognisable sounds could be heard like furniture scraping on the floor and human voices. A small flake of plaster fluttered down from the ceiling.

"Sounds like your sister is waking up. Perhaps she can help me. Was she in the car too?"

Lindsey stared at the notebook again, "No. She was here last night with her boyfriend. They were going to do some D.I.Y. upstairs this morning. They must have started already."

"Well, I'll leave it there for now," said WPC Foster as she stood up ready to go, "It's all right I can see myself out. Thank you for your help Miss Savage."

Lindsey went with her into the hallway, "I'll let you out because I have to be on my way too." As she opened the door there was a crash upstairs like a chair falling over.

"They sound as if they are working very hard."

"Yes they do, don't they," said Lindsey, glancing upwards as she very gently closed the door.

Chapter Fifteen

Making Plans

It was thirty minutes after midday when John woke up. Susan was still sleeping. She was lying on her side with her back to him. His eyes followed the curve of her spine and he remembered the painting of Venus by Valazquez in the National Gallery, "Only her hair is different. In the painting it's dark reddish-brown," he thought. Susan's hair was spilling over her shoulders and onto the pillow in a river of yellow. The fingertips of one hand rested on her shoulder where they held back some of her hair like a waterfall which moved very slightly on her back when she breathed. John was so overwhelmed with this vision that he kept perfectly still to keep her from waking while he realised that this was one of the moments in his life he would remember for ever.

Eventually he became aware that Susan was moving. She turned over, looked into his eyes and smiled.

"I love you," said John.

Susan's eyes seemed to double in size, "You said it! At last!"

"I did, didn't I? Without thinking about it. That's the trick with these things ....You probably think I'm ridiculous."

"No I don't. I think you're the most wonderful man on earth and I want us to have hundreds of babies together."

"What, all at once?"

"One to start with anyway."

"I'm sure that could be easily arranged madam..... Listen. I've been wanting to tell you I loved you ever since I met you, which is all of three days ago. It is ridiculous, I know it is, especially as I feel as if I've known you all my life, but I've never said it to anyone before. I've been feeling all awkward and gawky - exactly the same as when I was fifteen and forced myself to ask my first girlfriend to 'go out with me' as they used to say. 'You wanna go for a walk?' I think I said."

"Did you love her?"

"Not really, but she was very pretty and my mates told she really liked me - it was sort of like that. But here I am, twelve years later, and I'm really in love for the first time. It's fantastic but I've developed a bit of anxiety. I've become very aware that you are too valuable to lose."

"Fat chance. You're not going to get rid of me easily."

"On Saturday, yesterday I mean, I thought I saw you in the crowd at the football match and my heart started beating like mad. I was disappointed when it wasn't you but elated again when I thought how beautiful you were compared to her. Then in the evening when I thought I saw the digger smash you to bits I was terrified. It's been like a roller coaster ride, especially with that stuff by the canal on top of everything else. But when I woke up next to you just now it was the happiest I've ever been in my life!"

"Yes," said Susan slowly, "I think you are most definitely in love with me." She smiled, "Good, innit?"

"Very."

"Are you anxious now?"

"Not at all."

"Nor me. Hey, I know what I was going to ask you. Last night, just before Lindsey drove me home, I said, 'Why are you looking at me like that?' and you said you would tell me later. Tell me now please."

"Oh yes, I know. You called me John."

"What?"

"You never called me that before. It was as if we had been together for ages. Very sexy."

Susan climbed on top of him and held his hands down on the bed, "OK, JOHN. Come and get me, JOHN......" she leant down and blew in his ear....then whispered "… John... John .. John!"

John sat up and was about to kiss her when she giggled, jumped out of bed, trampled across the devastation that was her bedroom floor and grabbed her dressing gown. He chased her out of the room and across the landing until she locked herself in the bathroom. From behind the door she said, "We'd better get ready Mr. Street. I want to have some lunch before we go to Ben's place."

An hour later John was driving Susan in his car on the north road out of Hemel Hempstead. "Look, that's new," he said as they stopped opposite a large gap in the wood on the right hand side of the road. Through this opening there was a clear view of Ben's strange house with his weird machines and the dam, all bathed in unaccustomed sunlight resulting from the felling of so many trees. A makeshift road surface of broken bricks had been laid down so they were able to drive straight in to the property and down a slight slope to park next to the house. A terracotta cloud of dust followed them and was still hanging in the air as they got out of the car. Ben came towards them with a sheaf of papers in his hand which he waved about in a vain attempt to fan away the dust. They could hardly make out what he was saying until he came near and they caught the tail end of a great deal of cursing, "..stupid bloody bastards. Look what they've done to my place."

"Sorry about the dust," said John, "I didn't realise........"

"I wasn't raving on about you. I'm talking about the council. The dust doesn't matter. I meant to pour some water on it this morning but I haven't had time. It's good to see you both anyway," he said, shaking hands with John and kissing Susan. He gave the papers to Susan, "Look at all this stuff. All sorts of warnings and threats - mostly telling me to leave the property immediately while they demolish the buildings - for my 'own health and safety'. What a load of Jackson Pollocks. Anyway, on Friday my solicitor put some kind of prevention order on them. But it's only a delaying tactic. They are starting again on Friday week. By them I mean Croucher Demolition. Guess who Colin Croucher's sister is on the council."

"Not Mrs. Malaprop!" said Susan.

"The very same, and he's just the monster you would expect her brother to be. They should have everything flattened by Saturday week. The solicitor says they can't make me leave while it's still my property but I'm not allowed to 'interfere or hamper' the demolition work."

Susan put her arm round him, "I'm so sorry Ben. It must be awful for you."

"Well there you go. Nothing I can do about it- but I'm glad I can be here to stop them doing things they shouldn't. Look at all the trees they've cut down where you drove in. Mind you I don't object to that because there has to be a way in for vehicles. You'll need that won't you Susan?"

"Yes, that's true. So what exactly will be left, I mean what am I buying?"

"I'm selling you four acres of woodland with planning permission for a single dwelling. That's it. Pretty raw stuff. It'll be sad to see it all knocked down but I want you to have a clean start to build whatever you want. I told the council they have to pay for the demolition because I've got no money," he said with a wink.

"I think it's exciting. We'll be like pioneers, like early settlers in the Wild West."

Ben looked at John, "You said 'we'. Are you two a unit already? Are you buying this place together?"

Susan and John looked at each other. John spoke first, "We've talked about this, briefly. Yes we have become a very close couple, which is a bit of an understatement, but this is Susan's project entirely and she is going to buy it on her own but of course I'll be involved in it as much as she wants me to be. I am buying number one Herbert Street and we are both going to live there until this place is finished. After then who knows. It might be good to keep Herbert Street for rental income while I live here with Susan. I'm very relaxed about it and basically whatever Susan wants she can have."

Susan smiled at Ben, "There you are, I told you he was an OK guy, didn't I?"

"Shifty looking newspaper man I'd say! You know the sort."

"Is the dam staying?" asked Susan.

"Ah. I was just going to mention that. They said they were going to demolish that too but I'm going to fight to keep it. It does no harm and it's a haven for fish and other wildlife, especially the kingfishers..but.. .... you might be interested in the latest estimate from the electric company. I don't know why they hadn't thought of it before, but they now say they can run a cable from a much nearer substation and if they do, it will cost half as much, £15,000 instead of the £30,000 they quoted before. I know it's still a lot of money but it would increase the value of the property by much more than that."

"Mmmm," said Susan, "maybe, but let's try and keep the dam anyway."

"Oh yes," said Ben, "I will certainly try."

"Excuse me asking," said John, "but why didn't you make a vehicle access before?" Susan smiled because she knew what Ben was going to say.

"Because I don't have a car! And also in the beginning I didn't want people noticing what I was doing to the place, hence the path down a tunnel through the trees you discovered when you first came here. That path was wide enough for lorries once but after I finished my home I let it become overgrown again."

"I love that tunnel. It's like you're walking into a grotto," said John, "But how do you manage to get about without a car?"

"See that bicycle over there? Well, that takes me to the town centre very easily because it's a flat road and the bus stop is just over there on the edge of Gadebridge Park. For anywhere else I get a taxi or sometimes I hire a self-drive car or van. I always get those from a rent-a-heap place then no-one tries to steal them. It's much more economic for me than buying a car with tax and insurance and petrol and stuff. Besides which I don't have many possessions, apart from a few tools and this place. I don't have a watch or television or a camera even, would you believe. I've got my painting stuff of course but a few brushes and canvases aren't worth anything. Possessions tie you down and give you anxiety. By the way do you want any of the fixtures and fittings? They won't take those away if I tell them not to."

"What do you think, John? I wouldn't mind having the wood-burning stove and the solar panels. I'm sure we could use those."

"Definitely. Especially with all this woodland. There must be enough dead branches just falling on the ground to keep it going."

"Very nearly," said Ben, "But you'll find you're never short of firewood and there is always building going on somewhere and skips full of the stuff. You wouldn't like the treadmill would you?"

"Sorry," said Susan, "but tell me what you want for the other stuff and we'll pay you as soon as you like."

"Not a penny, I'll be very happy to see it put to good use....." he was interrupted by Susan's mobile telephone ringing.

"Hello. Yes ... he's just here.... Lindsey wants to talk to you, John."

"Hello Lindsey........... Oh yes how did it go with your fashion king? .... Yes, all right, I can do that. I have a very early job on Thursday but I'm free for the rest of the day. Is that soon enough? ....Of course, yes, you're coming to dinner in Hemel Thursday night anyway. Great. Just a minute I just want to ask Ben something." he held the phone away from his face so everyone could hear what was being said, "Lindsey says the buyer is very impressed and would like some photographs of the dresses. He doesn't want glossy magazine locations and expensive models just yet, he just wants some pictures to show his partners at their meeting next week. Can I borrow your studio Ben?"

"Of course. My pleasure. They won't be knocking it down for at least a week after you've finished with it."

"Thanks Ben," John turned to Susan, "The other thing Lindsey wants is for you to model the dresses - there will be ten of them. Is that OK?"

Susan nodded but took the phone from John, "Hello Sis, yes I'll do it - but you know I don't get out of bed for less than £5000 ! ......Of course I don't want anything. ...... what about you John.. and Ben? No, they're shaking their heads. OK next Thursday, ten o'clock in the morning. Talk to you before then." She handed the phone back to John.

"So that's all fixed ..... No, there's no need for prints. I'll e-mail the images to you and you can pick the best ones and send them to your man..... I'm fine. I'm looking forward to it....'bye.......She said to thank you, Ben, and she says she owes you one. Her voice is exactly the same as yours, Susan. Are you all right with being photographed? I was going to suggest Lindsey models the dresses - save you taking time off work."

"They won't know. I'll tell them I'm with a client, which is almost true, besides which Lindsey will want to fuss around with the clothes to make them look right. Anyway it will be interesting to see you at work. I've never seen you taking photographs."

"Not even in the marquee? No, that's right, you were hiding behind a cupboard door or something."

"You'll like the studio," said Ben, "Lots of daylight coming in through the big windows which face north so you won't get direct sunlight."

"Sounds perfect, thanks."

"We wanted to ask you something else. Can you come to dinner on Thursday night? It'll just be us three and Lindsey."

"I hate dinner parties- you know that."

"I know," said Susan, pointing a thumb at John, "He's another one. He has dining problems as well so I promise the food will be ready at seven thirty on the dot. So please come. We've been wanting to do something all together before you go to Spain."

"Just four of us you say?"

"Yes. Oh, and no dressing up, strictly come as you are, nothing smarter than a T-shirt and jeans, that's what I'm wearing anyway. Mind you 'come as you are' could mean anything with Lindsey. She'll probably come as a vampire bat or something."

"All right then. I'll come. Thank you. And don't worry about this place. It will be all yours as soon as the paper work is done. Listen though, can you remind your sister there's no smoking allowed here, especially in the studio."

"Don't worry. She's given up. She been to see a hypnotist and she's cured."

John raised his eyebrows, "She wasn't cured last night because I saw her having a fag. That's when I began to realise she wasn't you. Even then she had a hard job convincing me."

"Oh Lindsey, Lindsey! I'm not the most rigidly honest person in the world but my sister drifts into her own sort of reality whenever it suits her. She is probably convinced in her own mind that she's given up - even when she's lighting a cigarette. This is how she manages to do scary stunts and semi-dangerous stuff. She can take herself off into another world that suits her imagination whenever she feels like it. She doesn't even know she's doing it. Did I ever tell you about the incident with the cross on the church tower and the crane Ben? Never mind, I'll tell you when we're having dinner. She won't mind. I do love my sister despite what she's like. But yes I'll tell her about not smoking here."

They said their good-byes and as they drove up the brick road to the gate Susan turned round to look back at Ben standing all alone in the centre of his shabby kingdom. "It very sad," said Susan blowing her nose to hide her tears, "He's putting a brave face on it but I can tell he is very angry and upset."

"But he does know the property is going to end up in your safe hands - and my helping hands too."

"It's just that standing there looking all vulnerable he reminds me of my dad."

John stopped the car.

"Reminds you? Is he.. ?"

"He died three years ago. My mum was killed in an accident. A wall collapsed on her as she was walking home from the shops. She died instantly, wouldn't have known anything about it, so the hospital said. Hope they were telling the truth. My dad died a year later, from a broken heart really. They were so close."

"I'm so sorry."

"I'm all right most of the time, just little things trigger the memory sometimes, like just now. I meant to tell you ages ago. Trouble is we've either been having loads of fun or traumatic drama."

"That pretty well sums it up."

"It's so nice at the moment, with us I mean, we're very lucky."

"What do you mean luck? It's bloody hard work!" laughed John.

"I want us to be like my parents, only hopefully live a bit longer! They were so happy together."

"I suppose the loss of your parents explains why you

have a house in Herbert Street and Lindsey has a shop in Barnet?"

"Yes. And my brother, Andrew, has a house by the beach in Australia, and he and his partner, Bruce, have a chain of hairdressers in Perth."

"Wow. I know you would rather have your parents alive but they've provided for you all very well."

"Yes, bless them. What about your parents?"

"Well, I'm an orphan too would you believe."

"No! Really?"

"It's different to your story. My parents were killed in an earthquake in Japan twenty five years ago on a family holiday. The hotel collapsed. I was two years old and my brother, Wallace, was four. We survived because we were in a crèche at the side of the main building. Wallace remembers very little of our mum and dad and I have no recollection at all. We were brought up by wonderful adoptive parents in Portsmouth who spoilt both of us. They died of old age really, about ten years ago. Wallace, and I …by the way his name got shortened at school and my nickname was Fleet so we were Wall Street and Fleet Street.... Wallace and I came into a trust fund, set up by my parents' life insurance company, when we were each twenty one and that's how I'm able to buy your place. There you go."

"Poor little orphans then, aren't we."

"Only we're not poor."

"Good job innit. There's still no money around since the recession. It's very nice having secure homes but we still have to work to eat and there aren't many jobs about."

"Do you think our missing parents are another reason we're drawn to each other?"

"What, each feeling the other is the damaged too? Possibly. Are you getting all analytical again?"

"Not really. Hey, you said you were a second child like me. What about Lindsey?"

"I didn't. I said 'might be' and besides which I was born half a minute before my sister, so there, Mr. Smarty Pants."

Chapter Sixteen

The photo shoot

Thursday arrived after three days of torrential rain. The good people, and the not so good people of Hemel Hempstead woke to sunshine and a cloudless sky. At nine thirty that morning John noticed only one minor blemish in the heavens as a solitary airliner scratched a vapour trail high above him. He had just come from a very early job photographing a popular retiring milkman delivering his last bottles and now he was excited at the prospect of photographing Lindsey's dresses. He was slightly apprehensive too. *'I'd better make a damn good job of it. It's not like taking pictures for just anybody. This is a bit closer to home!'* He remembered Susan's words much earlier in the day when he woke her with a cup of tea, "I'm so happy for my sister. I hope it all goes well today. These photographs are going to mean so much to her." John had replied with a great show of confidence, "They'll be fantastic. No problem. Don't worry, I shall be taking this session very seriously indeed, but it'll be fun! See you later."

'Ah, well, I always take my best pictures when I'm slightly nervous', he thought to himself as he drove

carefully over the broken bricks down to Ben's house. As soon as he arrived Ben stepped off his veranda and ambled towards him. "Everything's ready for you. I went in early to open the sky-lights on the studio roof and let the heat out. It's quite pleasant in there now. Susan's there already trying on dresses."

"Susan? No Lindsey?"

"No. She came last night and put all the clothes on a rail in the studio but she phoned me this morning to say she has to meet a client. So it's just you and Susan."

John strode purposefully into the studio, dumped his camera bag on the floor and looked all around without saying a word. Standing by the clothes rail, made from a scaffolding pole slung from two ropes, was a familiar figure wriggling into a dress so that her torso and head were hidden from view. Eventually a familiar face appeared but with unfamiliar bobbed black hair. "Hello again," he said, taking test photographs of various parts of the room to prepare the camera.

"Do you like the wig? How do I look?"

"Don't worry, I'm quite immune to shocks now! Oh, I see, of course. It's to go with the dress." He put his camera on the floor for a moment and scrutinised his subject. The dress was the tan-coloured one with fringes that John last saw Lindsey wearing on Sunday morning. "So it's just us two," he said as he picked up the camera and walked to the middle of the studio.

"Sis has got to meet a client apparently - but we can do this by ourselves. Piece of cake!"

"As you say. Right, camera ready, action! Have you got a long string of beads to twirl round?"

"Ta-ra!" Some white beads were produced and John started taking photographs while his model attempted to dance little bits of the Charleston. He used fairly slow shutter speeds to blur the fringes on the dress and the beads to suggest movement.

"What do you think?" asked John as they looked at the images together at the back of the camera.

"Absolutely perfect. The fashion king is going to love those."

"OK next one!" demanded John good naturedly, "I don't pay you a thousand pounds an hour to hang about!"

"Yes sir. I'll be glad to get this wig off. It's ever so hot."

"Oooo, I know!," said John in a camp voice, "I'm absolutely boiling when I do my drag act."

They went very quickly through the dresses with both photographer and model making great efforts to produce the best possible images. The studio interior was simple but very practical. The ends of the room were plain walls, one painted black and the other white. The long wall opposite the giant windows was covered in mirrors from floor to ceiling like a dance studio but without the rail. John took photographs of light dresses against the black wall, dark dresses against the light wall, some with his model pretending to be asleep on the floor and finally front and back views at the same time in the giant mirrors. After three quarters of an hour there was just one left - the white tube towel. "I want to take the last shots of the towel thing outside by the water somewhere. That OK?"

"Fine by me. I'll get ready."

John wandered out into the grassy clearing and walked over to where the River Gade was pouring over the edge of the dam in a beautiful gushing waterfall after the heavy rains.

Ben appeared at his side, "Do you want a beer? No, you won't if you're driving, I remember."

"A glass of water would be lovely, I'm sweltering."

"OK. I can't give you much to eat but there's a basket of apples on my veranda. What will Susan want to drink?"

"The same I expect but I'll ask her... oh here she comes .... Water all right for you as well?"

"Yes please. Have you ever known it as hot as this in April? Please say you want to photograph me under the waterfall!"

"Well, close to it anyway." They walked together towards the dam. "I need to sit you on something."

Ben appeared with two glasses of water with ice cubes clinking on the surface.

"Have you got something she can sit on, Ben? I don't want her just standing in front of the waterfall."

"Steps?"

"How about a stool."

"Tell you what I have got. That marble pillar over there. It's hollow so it's not as heavy as it looks but you'll have to help me carry it." Twenty minutes later all three of them were looking in the back of the camera at splendid images of a young blond woman sitting by a waterfall on a marble pillar wearing what looked like a towel. In the photographs the towel seemed to stay in place by defying gravity as the model had both arms free - one hand dangling by her side while the other filled a glass with water sparkling in the sunshine.

"Aaaah ...," said all three of them."

"Very nice," said Ben, "Couldn't do better me self. I was a photographer once you know." They both ignored him, probably because he was muttering.

"Thank you Miss Savage," said John.

"Thank you, Mr. Street. Can you lend me a real towel, Ben? That water doesn't feel too cold and I want to have a swim in your lagoon up there if that's all right."

"Course you can," said Ben, walking off towards his house.

"Well done, by the way," said John as he put his camera bag into the boot of his car, "You're very easy to photograph."

"Thank you kind sir. It's interesting to see the way you work. You go all serious and you don't hang about do you?"

"Well, you can lose the moment dithering around while the model gets bored."

"Well I didn't get bored at all. It was exciting."

John adopted a semi-Cockney accent, "Yoo must 'ave done this before luv. Fancy breakin' into the modellin' business? I got a foo contacts......"

"Nah mate. Don't fancy it. 'Sides I got me other jobs ain't I ?"

Ben arrived with a towel, "Just be careful. It's very deep by the dam and only a metre by the bank."

"As long as no one can see me-I don't want to give anyone a heart attack!" The two men watched as she scampered up the steps at the side of the dam and disappeared. Less than a minute later they heard a shriek of delight followed by a splash, then, "Bloody hell it's cold!" Finally a dripping face with wet blond hair clinging to it's cheeks appeared on the top of the waterfall. "I lied! It's really lovely---or rather it's all right when you get used to it. Are you coming in?"

Ben walked back down to his house, "Not me, I've got to go into town. You'll have to share the towel John, that's the only clean one I've got." He grabbed his ancient bicycle and carried it over the broken bricks to the road. "See you tonight," he shouted as he disappeared from view.

In the grotto above the dam dappled sunlight filtered through the branches which already had tiny leaves and spring buds reaching down and almost touching the surface of the lagoon. It was quiet now with just the muffled sound of the water below the dam reaching the ears of the two bathers. A patch of sunlight illuminated two piles of clothes at the base of a tree and the solitary towel hanging on a branch. John was wading gingerly into the water. He glanced around, surprised to find himself apparently alone. He was slightly relieved that there was no witness to his less than macho attempts to immerse himself. Then, just as the water reached a suitable level for preserving his modesty, he spotted a mass of blond hair swirling below the surface as it came nearer and nearer. All John's hopes of gradual immersion were dashed as the water erupted in front of him. Seconds later the bathers were locked in a battle of frenzied splashing accompanied by shrieks and yells which sent all the birds around the lagoon into the air squawking their protests as they went. Even the heron, which had been perching unnoticed on the edge of the dam in hope of an early lunch, loped reluctantly into the air glaring over it's shoulder with a dark accusing eye.

John pursued his attacker across the lagoon until she rested with her elbows on the top of the dam. He adopted the same position next to her. After he had recovered his breath John was the first to speak, "We'll have to stop them knocking this down. It's a little bit of paradise. You'd think we were hundreds of miles from Hemel Hempstead."

"I know. It really is a magical place."

John moved a little closer with the intention of kissing her shoulder just above the water line, "You're so clever to find it."

"What? No not really. I've been here before. Susan showed me round once..... What's the matter?" John was staring at her shoulder where he could see a small part of a scorpion tattoo where the water had washed off some of the covering make-up. "Oh no! she laughed, "You thought I was Susan didn't you." John said nothing and began swimming back to the bank. Lindsey followed him, "I'm sorry! I'm sorry," she shouted, "I thought you knew who I was."

When John was nearly at the water's edge he spoke to Lindsey without looking at her. "Would you mind looking the other way while I get out?"

She complied with his request but carried on talking with her back turned, "All right but don't you think it's a bit late for that now," she said, trying not to giggle, unsuccessfully, "Look, nothing happened. We can forget all about it if you like."

"You might be able to forget it but I won't be able to, and what happened to promising not to play tricks on me and that bit about making it clear which one of you is which?"

"It wasn't a trick honestly. You have to believe me."

"All right. Maybe when I was taking pictures you might have thought that I knew who you were but what about when I came up here? Didn't you think it was a strange way for your sister's boyfriend to behave?"

"Can I turn round now?"

"Yes."

"Now you look the other way, please, while I get out."

"OK. I've left more than half of the towel dry for you."

"Thank you. My, my, now I'm the one being ever so modest aren't I ?" said Lindsey as John stood gazing at the trees. "All right yes, I was surprised when you came up here for a swim - a tiny bit shocked actually. That's why I hid myself away when I saw you arrive and begin to strip off. But then I thought, 'What the heck. I don't mind - if he doesn't.' Anyway it was all quite innocent. You didn't try anything did you."

"No, but I might have done! That's the whole point."

"Well sorry and all that but it's not my fault OK?"

"Of course it's not your fault. No one's to blame. Mind you what about Ben? He said you phoned him this morning to say you couldn't come because you had to meet a client. And I distinctly remember him saying that Susan was here already, trying on dresses."

"I think that was a genuine mistake. Susan must have phoned him. She's the one meeting a client. We sound exactly the same and, now I come to think of it, he called me Susan this morning. I didn't take any notice because I get used to people saying it all the time. You can turn round now if you want."

John turned round, walked back to the tree and stood with one arm hooked over a branch. His self-confidence had returned and he was able look Lindsey in the eye, "So where do we go from here? I really want us to be friends, but we need to talk about this."

"I agree. I would hate it if we didn't get on." They began to move down past the dam keeping almost exactly one metre apart as they walked. When they reached the grassy clearing John pointed with his thumb at the veranda, "Do you want to sit here for a bit before we go?"

"Yes, now is good. Susan said 'now' is your favourite word."

"Do you know everything about me?"

"Pretty much, but nothing I don't like."

Lindsey sat in Ben's rocking chair while John sat next to her on a beer crate. They maintained the unspoken distance rule of one metre apart. Lindsey spoke first, "Lets face it. It's pretty obvious that you are going to find me physically attractive because I look exactly like my sister. But that shouldn't be a problem for either of us. You're not a machine or a randy Labrador. If you see Susan's reflection in a mirror you're not going to lust after it just because it looks like her. Well in much the same way I'm not like Susan either. There are lots of differences between us besides the tattoo on my shoulder. Susan might not be perfect but I can tell you she's an angel compared to me. I'm a much harder person - and more dishonest, honestly!" she laughed, "No, I'm not a habitual liar or anything I'm just, er, irresponsible with the truth. In fact that's a good word for me, I'm just irresponsible. It's a good job you and me are not a unit. It would be hopeless. If you don't mind me making a personal guess I think you're the sort that would like to have children. You don't have to answer that, it's none of my business, although it might be one day! Anyway I don't want any kids. I just wouldn't want the hassle and quite frankly I'm sure I would be a lousy mother. Susan loves children. I don't hate them and if you two happened to make loads of nephews and nieces for me I would be delighted. I could come and visit - 'Crazy Aunt Lindsey's coming to stay', - oh no! can you imagine the scene?"

"Yes I can," laughed John, "but I'm sure you'd be their favourite aunt. Do you want an apple? Ben said to help ourselves."

"Thank you."

Instead of offering all the apples he selected the best one, picked up a knife from the table, and, in five swift movements cut it in half, cut the centre out of each half, put the two halves back together again and offered her a core-less apple. "There you are. Eat it quick before it goes brown."

"Thanks. Are you trying to impress me or is this the forbidden fruit to seduce me with?"

"No. Do you think I'm the serpent? OK, in the spirit of openness and stuff are you going to say what you think I'm like?"

"Get you. You're so confident asking me that aren't you, you smug bugger. You and your heroism with hooray Henrys and core-less apples." She looked directly into his face for a few seconds, "Well, you're too nice for me I think. I don't mean you're a softy but I would have a hard job having a row with you without having loads of guilt. You're not fantastically good looking but not many blokes are unless they are gay or womanisers. What are you laughing at?"

"It's just that's just what I say sometimes."

"There you are. Great minds and all that. You're not homophobic are you?"

"Not at all, and it's all right Susan told me about your brother. I'm looking forward to meeting him."

"OK next. You have nice hands. Nice people have nice hands. Horrible people have horrible hands. You ever seen photos of Hitler's hands? They're just like a bunch of limp sausages. I study body language an awful lot and I talk too much as well so when I'm at a lousy party, you know the sort, where it's so bad anybody with half a brain ends up in the kitchen nibbling cubes of cheese on sticks desperate to listen to anybody with something to say, well this is

147

when I start talking about body language. I mention that people who feel insecure and defensive stand with their arms folded, which they nearly all are of course. At which point, mostly the men, very, very slowly unfold their arms and hope nobody notices. Then I mention the hands bit and everybody, I mean everybody, put their hands in their pockets or if they haven't got those they put their hands behind them. It's great fun. Especially if you've already told a mate that you're going to do it." She paused.

"Is that it? I've got nice hands."

"Yeah. That's about it. Can't think of anything else. You're OK for a bloke I suppose which is meant to be a compliment. I don't like many men. They're usually like little boys, only they grow big and get hairy bits and go bald, smell of sweat, become aggressive and take it out on the world by playing cricket or driving like idiots," she paused again, "You're laughing. Is that because you agree with me or you think I'm a bitch?"

"Bit of both, no, wouldn't say bitch. I would like to think of you as forthright, headstrong, determined, that sort of thing," he said jokingly.

"Now you're talking like a drip. On the other hand you must be all right if Susan chose you."

"You make it sound like going to Sainsbury's."

"A woman always chooses the man. Of course he has to be interested in her first and she will let him think he is doing the wooing."

"I like to think it was mutual with Susan and me."

"Do you now? OK how far do you think you would have got with her if she wasn't interested?"

"Nowhere."

"There you are then."

"But what if I wasn't interested?"

148

"Nothing would have happened. But you were interested so it did happen."

"How is that different from being mutual."

"Look, it's simple. How many attractive female admirers did you have to choose from?"

"…...Not many."

"And how many male admirers do you think Susan had?" no answer, "There you go."

Silence for thirty seconds then John said, "Oh well if you're right it seems to work - works for me anyway. I'm thinking of a mate of mine who only thinks of one thing, two things, to be exact, he would fall in love with a lamp post if it had large breasts. If the choice was left to him anything could happen."

"So what do you think of me?"

"I think you have described yourself so perfectly that's what you're like as far as I'm concerned. I'm sure you are being honest with me too. If you do that with me all the time I will be a great friend to you."

"What I mean is do you like me?"

"Yes, a lot."

"Good."

"Look. Up there in the pool I wasn't angry with you. I was angry with the situation and myself for not being aware of who you were and not taking the trouble to check. It was because I was concentrating on taking photographs I expect."

"Speaking of which," said Lindsey as she stood up, "what happens now? When will you e-mail them to me?"

"I'll need to edit out some of the rubbish shots and tweak the images a bit but I'll send them to you later this afternoon. Where will you be?" They were making their way round to where their cars were parked. By now they had abandoned the one metre rule and were walking quite close to each other. Lindsey opened the boot of her car.

"I'll be at my shop in Barnet till five. I've got to take the dresses back now."

"Of course, this is your car. I thought it was Susan's for some reason."

"She'll be driving the estate agent's car today." They turned to look at each other.

"What shall we tell her?" asked John.

"What do you mean, we? Sounds like we've been caught behind the bike sheds. You tell her what ever you want. I'm not going to tell her anything unless she asks but if she does I'll tell her the truth."

"So will I."

"Good."

"Do you want a hand?"

"No... Yes, if you like. Thank you." They loaded up the car in silence. When they had finished she sat in the driver's seat and wound down the window. "See you tonight then, half past seven."

"On the dot." They were still looking at each other. Lindsey got out of the car, put her arms round his neck and kissed him on the cheek, "You do nice things with apples," she whispered. As she drove away she passed Ben on the broken brick road. He lifted his bicycle and shopping bag to one side to avoid the red dust cloud. "Hello John. What do you think?" He held up a brand new pair of jeans and a striped T-shirt. "I didn't want to look like an old tramp this evening and my other clothes are ancient."

"I think you'll look great."

"Well us male models have to keep up appearances."

John's mobile phone rang. "Hello Susan... No, we were fine. Got some really good pictures. I'll show you them later on. Lindsey thinks they're great. I just hope her client likes them too............. No, she's already gone back to her place with the dresses so we'll see her at dinner..... I'm sorry, I always switch my phone off when I'm snapping. Can I do anything - to get ready I mean. ....All right. I'll nip into the bakers on the way. I'm going to Herbert Street now..... Not half as much as I missed you. See you soon."

"Was that Lindsey driving out the gate?" asked Ben.

"Yes"

"Sorry. I might have misled you. That must have been her you were photographing today. I just can't tell them apart."

"Tell me about it!" said John, as he got into his car, "See you tonight."

Chapter Seventeen

The Dinner Party

John was sitting at the dining room table at Herbert Street. He had showered and changed and was more relaxed now that he had got rid of the slight smell of river water that he had noticed as he was driving home. He regarded number one Herbert Street as his home now and liked the feeling it gave him. He had laid the table ready for four people by means of foraging in cupboards for plates, cutlery and glasses as a token measure of helping. Now he was busy with his laptop burning the finished images of his morning's work onto a disc. He got up when he heard a key turning the lock in the front door and met Susan in the hallway.

"Hello you," she said as she kissed him.

"Hello yourself. How was your meeting?"

"I've only just got rid of him. He wanted to see loads of properties and then I had to do a valuation on his place …. he was just a complete arse that's all. Never mind that. Let's see the pictures then!"

John led her into the dining room and sat down next to her. After a while she exclaimed, "Wow! They're good John. Oh yes, John!" she said, and blew into his ear. "Was it difficult with just the two of you?"

"It wasn't too bad because I showed her the images as we went along and she didn't have to fiddle with the dresses......," He stopped because Susan put a finger on his lips.

"You went skinny-dipping with my sister."

"Oh bloody hell!" exploded John as he turned bright red and stood up, talking at high speed, "I didn't know it was her! Ben said she was you and she'd covered up her tattoo and I was too interested in taking pictures and anyway she should have told me...."

"OK. OK. It's all right. I believe you. As you might have guessed Lindsey told me this afternoon. She said that it was a mistake and nothing happened and you behaved like a perfect gentleman. She wasn't going to say anything but I could tell something was on her mind. She couldn't lie to me, it would be impossible. Would you have told me?"

"It wouldn't have been easy, not because there was anything wrong, actually because there was nothing wrong. I thought you might say, 'Why are you telling me then?' if that makes sense."

"It does, and I would have."

"Oh."

Susan kissed him on the lips, "The only thing I'm sorry about is that I wish it had been me. Mind you it must have been cold!"

"It was a bit."

"Thanks for laying the table, oh, and getting the bread rolls."

"What are you going to cook?"

"Cook? Not me. Well not tonight anyway. We're having Taiwanese takeaways. Here's a list of what everyone wants so ring this number please, and tell them what you'd like as well. The meals are all the same price and I've paid for them already. Ask them to deliver at ten past seven. What time is it now?"

"Nearly half past six."

"OK, I'm nipping in the shower."

"I saw Ben earlier. He's only gone and bought jeans and a T-shirt for this evening."

"Wow. We're honoured. He'll be ironing his jeans next. Maybe he's had a wash and shave as well! I so glad he's coming. He seldom does any socialising. You two can swap photographers' anecdotes."

"He'll have hundreds more than me. What can I do down here?"

"You can do arty things with the napkins and shove them in the glasses - oh, and put the bowls and plates in the oven to warm in ten minutes. Thanks."

John did as he was told then found he had time enough to stand and stare out of the window. He glanced at the sun which was now low enough to hide itself behind the spire of Hemel Hempstead's ancient Norman church. Near the weathercock a sparrow hawk was having a Battle of Britain dog fight with two crows. When the crows had seen off the hawk they returned to their airfield amongst the gravestones to feast noisily on a discarded bag of chips. *'I'm getting hungry too'*, thought John. There came a loud knock at the door.

"Four persons' dinner for Miss Savage?" said a young woman as she took four enormous bags from an insulated box.

"Thank you," said John giving her a tip.

"Let me help you with those," said Ben as he locked his bicycle to the lamp post.

"Hello Ben! You won't have to worry about drinking

and driving then. Thanks," he added as Ben handed him two bottles of wine, "Come in, come in. Glad you could come. We feel honoured."

"So you should." he joked, "Hello Susan," he said as he kissed her on the cheek while she took the bags from him, "and I thought you would be slaving over a hot stove."

"Not me. We have employed outside caterers, don't-y-know. I like your T-shirt Ben. Come through and have a beer," said his hostess. John was just closing the door when Lindsey shouted, "No wait for me! I want to come in as well please."

"What do you look like sis?" Her sister was wearing a huge T-shirt which looked like it was made of a Hessian sack. It even had 'Harper's Barley Grains' printed on it upside down and it was just long enough for her to wear as a dress. Her hair was back-combed so much it resembled exploded candy-floss.

"Come as you are, you said. Well I was trying to disarm a bomb in a grain store."

"I think you are the height of elegance," said Ben.

"Thank you kind sir. You may take my arm and escort me into dinner."

One hour later the setting sun was turning the ceiling red above the diners as they drank their coffee. They were very relaxed and just as happy to listen as they were to take turns at relating stories and ideas. "All right then, Mister Ben Carter," Lindsey was saying with mock severity, "if you know so much about local history, how do you think that woman's skeleton ended up in Snook's grave."

"Abigail you mean. It's pretty certain that's her name by the way. A solicitor has got hold of some pretty amazing documents with details of what happened when Snook was executed," he held up the palms of his hands towards his friends in a gesture of apology, "I'm afraid I can't tell you an awful lot because for one thing Dr. Salter asked me not to and the other reason is that the story of Abigail and Snook would take too long to tell this evening, but..." he paused to let their groans and protests subside, "..... I can tell you three things. One; We now know that they were connected. Everyone assumed that but now it's confirmed. Two; That was not Snook's coffin. It was intended to be but obviously that didn't happen. Three; Dr. Salter is very soon going to start digging again with the hope of finding Snook's remains.

Four; You don't know about this because you weren't at work today, John, but at ten o'clock tomorrow morning there will be an editorial meeting in your office. I'll be there and so will Dr. Salter who will be telling the editor and his staff, including you, about the latest discovery. That's it. That's all I'm going to tell you. Sorry and all that."

"Wow! I can't wait for tomorrow." said John.

"How exciting!" said Susan. "You're so lucky, John. Can I come too?" she asked Ben.

"No. And no one knows about this meeting except the editor, Dr. Salter, and us four, but, if you promise not to say anything to anybody before next Wednesday, when the Gazette is published, I don't see why John can't tell you all about it tomorrow night. Yes it is exciting but, inevitably, when you think about it, the story is bound to be a rather sad one," he looked up at the others' watchful faces, "To change the subject completely, Susan, you said you were going to tell me the story of Lindsey and the cross and the church tower."

"Do you have to?" exclaimed Lindsey, All right I'm going to the loo. You can humiliate me when I'm not here."

As she left the room Susan began, "Lindsey and I went to different secondary schools. This was our parents' idea because they wanted us to grow up as separate people as much as possible. It worked very well at first and, although the schools were both less than a mile from our home in Buckinghamshire, we grew up with our own sets of friends and, as you might have noticed, with slightly different personalities. The main problem was with my sister and her school. This was at the time when we reached adolescence and we were both rebellious and downright anti- everything for a while. Lindsey's school was a faith school, a Christian one. I'm not going to say which denomination because it's still a good school which produces loads of well-educated and well behaved pupils. My sister's rebellion manifested itself by her becoming an outright atheist which was tolerated for a while in the interests of encouraging free thought I suppose, but Lindsey, being Lindsey, pushed things a bit too far. She refused to go to assembly, which was accepted, and she drove her R E teacher almost insane, which wasn't. The crunch came when she started to dress up as Jesus Christ, complete with beard, at every opportunity, at her birthday party, then art and drama projects and then on the school charity walk carrying a cross which got her into a lot of trouble. What resulted in her actually getting expelled was the incident with the crane. The head teacher, governors and benefactors were very proud of the church, complete with square tower, which was inside the school grounds. Various worthy people and charities donated money so that the church could have a new cross put on the top. The whole school, the mayor, governors, and local press gathered to watch the cross being lifted by crane to the top of the tower. So the crane started up, the cable was lowered to an area behind a fence and began lifting the cross accompanied by great cheering and waving from the crowd. But this died away suddenly. My sister, I don't know how, she's never told me, managed to persuade the crane workers to hoist her up on the cross and lift her gently to the top of the church tower ...."

"It was great fun, very spiritual," said Lindsey, who was leaning against the door frame and watching the men's faces, "It was so nice looking down at the awe-struck crowd. I was going to give them some kind of blessing but I thought I that might cause offence."

"Didn't you think you might have done that already?" asked John.

"Yes of course. That was the whole point of doing it," she said proudly, "Anyway, I stepped off the cross onto the roof and ran down the bell tower steps. I had my school uniform on underneath the sheet and beard so on the way down I stuffed them into a hole in the wall, ran round the back of the church and mingled with the crowd. The verger found the beard and sheet and gave them to the head teacher who'd already guessed it was me. So that was the end of my church school education. I thought the whole idea of Christianity was to forgive people but it didn't work for me."

"What about your parents?" asked Ben.

"Well, by then they were convinced I was bonkers-I was fifteen by the way - and I don't think anything I could have done would have surprised them. They forgave me, which is nice, without even being religious." She sat down in her seat next to Ben, "Do you have a religion?" she asked him.

"Sort of. No I don't. I could never be religious but I like Zen Buddhism."

"Don't they have to wear robes and chant things to get to Nirvana."

"That's more Buddhist monks who are a lot different. I'm just interested in Zen applied to art and stuff."

"Excuse me but isn't that a load of pretentious rubbish?" asked Susan.

"Could well be, especially when a lot of pseudo intellectuals go on about it, but the bit that interests me is the way Zen holds spontaneous actions to be so important. They encourage their followers to do things without any pre-thinking whatsoever."

"Shall I spontaneously pour this jug of water over Susan's head?" asked John.

"Ah, but that wouldn't be spontaneous because you thought about it," said Susan, "Also, be careful, you might set Lindsey off and she'll start throwing plates out of the window or something."

"I know it sounds completely nutty until you try it," said Ben, "I do a lot of running which helps my creativity enormously. I'm sure this is because I'm doing something without thinking about my actions. It works especially well if I just go out of the door into the countryside without any idea of where I'm going to run to. It certainly works with figure drawing where you should aim to concentrate ninety five per cent on what you are looking at and five per cent on actually drawing. If you can do it, which happens with me sometimes, you finish a drawing, put it down and go for a coffee break , and when you come back you can hardly recognise it as your own work and you will have little or no memory of doing the actual drawing. The other thing which is very Zen, I think, is humour. Zen teachers ask their pupils unsolvable riddles which are supposed to convey how useless it is to 'use words to express the Absolute.' Now, just think how much truth is conveyed by humour, Monty Python stuff especially and the most Zen books ever written, I think, are Alice in Wonderland and Alice Through the Looking Glass. All right they're children's books but all adults should read them later in life. The insight you get of the madness of Victorian life and how it must have appeared to a young girl is just incredible to me.

What about you, Susan, what about your spiritual side?"

"I don't think I have one. Mind you I sometimes think it would be very comfortable to be religious and have everything sorted so you don't have to think any more, especially being blessed for being good. When I see people coming happily out of churches and things I think how nice it must be for them, like being children in your pyjamas and drinking cocoa in front of the fire while someone reads you a story. Sadly that wouldn't work for me now. But I am totally amazed by what I see, hear and feel and what I read and learn on TV and the internet. I've no idea why people want to believe in miracles when all they have to do is open their eyes and just look at what there is. I suppose it's because so very few people actually become grown up, whatever that means, and they still want to have some magnificent parent-being to make things all right for them. It's because we spend our lives being scared of dying I suppose. Animals don't have worries like that, probably because they have no reason to believe that they are going to do anything else but live for ever. When they get old they might be aware that they have a bit of pain and they can't move around so quickly but they probably think, just supposing for a moment they can think, that they're just a bit poorly and they'll be all right soon if they just keep on eating the grass or whatever they do. And then the miracle thing, just suppose I was able to point to that glass, raise my finger and make it float in the air. It would be extremely interesting and outside of our conception of what's normal but a miracle no. Not compared with all the other miraculous things that we take for granted, like gravity which pulls on it so that it stays on the table, like the stuff it's made of that you can see through and of course the molecules and atoms that keep the thing together long enough for us to pick it up and drink out of it."

"Shame," said Ben, "Just for a moment there I thought you were going to show us a fantastic trick."

"If I had done a trick you might have been amazed for a moment but then you would've wanted to know how it was done and if I gave you an explanation you would be bored and then you would forget all about it. So much for miracles. Anyway I'm not a complete atheist like Lindsey. I don't believe in a supreme being or anything but if there was such a thing I would be really, really, scared."

"Why?" asked John.

"Well, just let's think of our planet for a moment, and imagine that this supreme being had somehow overseen the start of life on earth and watched it evolve into human beings. I imagine that He, She, It, would be rather like someone who bred wonderful creatures in a huge aquarium with balanced oxygenating plants and well-behaved animals. Supposing He goes on holiday and comes back to find the tank overrun with little hairless creatures on two legs who are breeding too fast, destroying the plants and other animals and turning the water into foul stuff with hardly any oxygen. I mean what would you do?"

"Fish them out with a net and chuck them in the bin I suppose," said John, "Mind you if I found four delightful creatures like us blamelessly having their dinner I would put them back in the tank again and tell them to be good little souls from now on!" Susan punched him on the shoulder while the others laughed.

"Just a minute," said Lindsey, "while we're talking about humans and how they are supposed to be evolving, well something has gone very wrong in recent years. I mean if it's all about the survival of the fittest and the selfish gene and all that, why have we got complete idiots in charge of everything? I know it's always been a bit that way, 'lions led by donkeys' in the first world war and people like Emperor Nero, but surely it's never been as bad as it is in this country at the minute. I mean look at them all! Politicians, bankers, public transport bosses, why do we allow such incompetent people into management? Don't worry they're rhetorical questions. No one knows the answer and meanwhile everyone sits on their hands and does nothing."

"Let me know when the revolution starts," said Ben, "I'll give it my full support. I think we need a leader, a few leaders actually, to shake everyone out of their complacency. Someone like Churchill would do. People didn't want to listen to him when he warned them about Hitler. They wanted it all to go away with a bit of appeasement and general niceness all round. I remember my grandparents saying how relieved they were when Chamberlain came back with his famous piece of paper. The only thing that will save the world, environmentally

I mean, is for everything to be put on a war-time footing. Dig for victory, real tax incentives for solar panels and smaller cars. I HATE gas-guzzling private cars."

John spoke next, "I pretty much agree with all of you, especially the Zen thing with photography. My best photographs seem happen without any effort but the most difficult ones, like a portrait of an ugly person who really doesn't want to be photographed, nobody really appreciates."

"There, there. You poor old thing," said Susan.

"I shall ignore that hurtful remark," he said cheerfully, "One of my pictures that everyone seems to like is of a deer leaping across the windscreen of my car. 'How on earth did you get that?' they ask. Well , sort of like the Zen bit, it was very simple. I was driving through Ashridge forest and I noticed that the oncoming traffic had all stopped. So I stopped to see what was happening. Out of the trees came about twenty young deer running and jumping across the road just in front of my car. I had my camera on the passenger seat already switched on for the next job, so all I had to do was pick it up and fire away at all the deer as they passed in front of me. Dead easy. Everyone thinks that it was just one deer and that I had lightning reactions. I don't usually tell them anything else, spoils the illusion.

I also like Susan's aquarium analogy. We humans think we're so important. Of course we are pretty amazing creatures but not compared with everything else in the universe. Apparently there is eighty-five per cent more matter around than the stuff we can observe and measure and we have no idea what it is. It's extremely arrogant for humans to think that they are the only so-called intelligent beings that exist. I get fed up with people talking with great reverence about 'the sanctity of life' especially when they are condemning euthanasia. What they mean is human life. Well, of course, we're humans so we're bound to think our lives are important, but they're not really. But that doesn't mean we should stop living life to the full. We should be doing good stuff instead of messing up the aquarium."

"Talking of lives," said Lindsey, leaning back in her chair to stretch her arms and then messing up her hair even more with her hands, "You know this bit about time flying by, kind of like, 'Oh my God summer's over already and I haven't done so and so,' and how much we waste time by moaning and doing the wrong things or doing nothing at all and coming to the end of our lives too quickly and dying, well, wouldn't it be nice if we were dead nearly all the time but now and again we had a day of life, you know, like if you were a very expensive car that was only put on the road now and again. We would appreciate things so much more wouldn't we? And life would seem to go on for ever but we wouldn't have time to get bored!"

"That would be wonderful ," said Ben, "but it seems a bit difficult to arrange and don't we sort of do that already when we go to sleep every night? By the way I think this the strangest dinner conversation I've ever had. If somebody put this in a novel no one would ever believe it."

"Well," said Susan, raising her glass, "Here's to us and our futures."

"Hear hear!" and, "Cheers!" said everyone else.

"What about your future Ben?" asked John, "What are you going to do in Spain?"

"I've got a contract to teach English and portrait

painting in a small Catalan town near Barcelona. I am learning Spanish, very slowly, and my children and grandchildren will come and visit me and so will you lot I hope. I shall paint beautiful portraits of Spanish faces and go to friendly bars in the evening and talk and drink too much and grow old very ungracefully. What about you two?" he said to Susan and John.

"We," she looked at John for permission to speak for both of them, "We are going to build a beautiful home on your land, when it's ours, and be organic and environmentally friendly and keep chickens, and a sheep as a pet and let it grow old. I want to open a garden centre too. I know it's not fashionable, but I don't want a career. John will become a really successful photographer so I can stop work. Then I would like to have lots of children but we would have to sell an awful lot of trees to offset the carbon footprint."

"I confirm all that," said John, "but I do have a dream of what I would like do as well as all that bliss. Don't laugh but I would like to write a science fiction book. I love science fiction, not the modern stuff which seems to be ordinary stories; only set on Mars or on a spaceship or somewhere. To me that's not science fiction. My story is going to be about the occupants of one of a pair of binary planets. I'm sure you know about binary stars which spin round each other in a small shared orbit. Well my planets do the same but they also orbit together round their sun," he noticed their puzzled faces so he explained more, "Look, imagine if our moon was the same size as Earth we would probably be spinning round each other in an equal way rather than us keeping still while the moon goes round us. Anyway, in my story there is life on both planets but only human-like animals on one of them. They have developed

165

technology which is getting very nearly good enough to beat the gravitational pull of their home planet. For many years they have studied the other planet which is covered in oceans and rain forests and they rather hope that it is a Garden of Eden waiting for them. It would be similar to discovering the Americas only they can see where they are going. Both planets are spinning so they have tides twice a day and frequent lunar, or rather planetary, eclipses. Wars between nations have temporarily ceased because now all political and economic interest is focused on the new world but of course this is about to change.............. What do you think, does it grab you as an idea?"

"Well I'll want to read it anyway," said Ben, "Mind you, getting a publisher is the problem always. Ten years ago I wrote a novel set in Hemel. No publisher will even look at new work unless you have a reputation. But I don't care, my friends and family like reading it."

The doorbell rang.

"You expecting someone?" asked John.

"No. How exciting," said Susan, and went out to answer the door. Her guests could just hear another voice, a female one, then Susan, "You had better come in then. Perhaps one of the others knows why you're here." She opened the dining room door for her unexpected guest who burst into the room.

"Coo-ee! It's me, Nell Gwyn again. The King has given me a night off - but I'd rather 'ave a knight-on if yer know what I mean." Ben and John squirmed with embarrassment but forced themselves to smile - like carnival masks. "It's lovely to see young people like you taking in 'omeless dahn-and-ahts and giving 'em a bit of food," she said, pointing at Ben. She came close to him and bent down, "How do you like me oranges luv?

They're nice an' juicy, you can feel 'em if yer like," she elbowed him in the ribs, "but at your age I wouldn't want to give you a heart attack!" she shrieked and added her machine gun laugh. She turned to a terrified John next, "An' what do we 'ave here? The answer to every maiden's prayer - but not for me. I'm not praying for a glass of water and a good night's sleep." She moved in close and John withdrew so much he was back-arching in his chair. "Ello he's gorn all stiff. Catch 'im while you can ladies. I bet it don't 'appen very orften!" She turned on Lindsey, "My gawd what 'appened to you? You're not a vet are yer? Looks like you were looking up an elephant's arse when it farted," another machine gun laugh, "Nah then. It's time for me special message." She unrolled a sheet of beige paper and cleared her throat with a tiny cough.

"I 'umbly ask your gracious pardons all
  For my most inhorspicious wit an' all.
  I tried you gentle people to enthral
  But sadly drove your men-folk up the wall
  An' so before your revels start to pall
  I'd better take my leave from one and all
  An' take my fruit and button up my shawl
  An' thank you for your gifts however small!"

Only don't bovver wiv the gifts. I've been paid already." She gave a curtsey with arms spread wide, "I make me poems up as I go along - to fit the occasion." There was enthusiastic applause from her tiny audience and obvious relief from Ben and John.

"Thank you so much," said Susan,"but who asked you to come?"

"She wouldn't say. Said it was to be a surprise."

Everyone looked at Lindsey.

"What?" she said, her face a picture of innocence, "As if I would."

"I'd better go," said 'Nell Gwyn', "I've got two more of these to do and I don't think they will be as easy as you lot."

"Be careful," said Susan.

"It's all right. Craig comes with me. He's waiting in the car."

"How did you two meet?" asked Susan.

"I met him in the hospital after... you know."

"Are you a nurse?"

"Oh no luv! I was waiting in the A and E with me mum and her broken ankle. He let us go in front of him. He's ever so kind really. Goodbye everyone." They all said their farewells and Susan opened the door. Craig waved from the car. "He's a lovely man."

Susan returned to her guests, "I'll get you for that one day Sis!" she said jokingly.

"Oh I don't know," said John, "It's nice to have a good squirm now and again. What do you think Ben?"

Ben was looking serious but he smiled happily enough, "Sorry. I was thinking of something else. I didn't mind her really. I just don't know what to do on these occasions. She's very funny actually. I liked her daft poem, added a bit of culture to the evening."

"Me too," said Lindsey," My turn please. I want to tell you about my future." Her speech was becoming very slightly slurred now, as was everyone else's. Her fellow diners had drunk three glasses of wine each and were now beginning to feel their cheeks tightening up as they smiled. John offered everyone a fourth glass. Lindsey leant forward on her elbows to be illuminated by one of the spotlights in the ceiling behind her. This back-lit her crazy hair and for a moment she looked almost angelic. "Thank you," she said, looking up at John as he filled her glass, "I, Lindsey Savage, have decided to get married," .....sensation amongst her companions..... "to the most wonderful man I've ever met. He doesn't know it yet. Nobody does, because I've only just realised how I feel," she paused to dip two fingers into her glass of wine and put them in her mouth. She closed her eyes then opened them again to look at Susan and Ben in turn. She turned her middle finger round and round in her glass as she went on, "He has a partner already, but that doesn't matter. He thinks he loves her. He doesn't realise how he feels about me yet but he's going to soon. He's a skilled professional with a great future. I've seen him at work at close quarters recently and that's when it happened. I couldn't help falling in love. He just makes me feel as if I'm the only person in the world worth talking to. I found myself telling him things I've never said to anyone before. I just couldn't help it. Anyway I've decided to marry him. It's for his own good."

"Hey sis, that sounds a bit weird, like you are going to start stalking him."

"Don't be daft. I wouldn't do that. I'm just going let it happen."

"Well? Tell us who it is then?" demanded Susan.

Lindsey paused for dramatic effect, "He's Adam White, my hypnotherapist," John took a large mouthful of wine. He was sure everyone heard him swallow it, "he helped me stop smoking. If he can do that I think he could do anything. That's the last cigarette I ever had, you know John, when I first met you in this house."

"It seems ages ago," said John. He coughed slightly

and had to wipe some wine from his chin "Do you still want to smoke?"

"I'd be lying if I said no. But it's not so bad. It's like being hungry all the time but I forget what for. That's hypnotism for you. But it only works if you really want to give up."

"I hope it works for you," said Ben as he stood up, "Mark Twain said, 'It's easy to give up smoking, I've done it many times!' Thank you so much. I've had a lovely evening and I wouldn't have missed the conversations for anything!" Susan and John got up to see him to the door. Ben kissed Lindsey, with difficulty because of her hair, "God, it's like kissing a butterfly stuck in a spider's web," he said affectionately.

"Ah well that's a better compliment than Nell Gwyn's. You don't mind if I stay here do you? I think if I stand up I'll knock something over."

At the front door Susan said, "Thank you for coming. How are you feeling, you know, about your place? I was going to ask you before but you were having such a good time I didn't want to mention it."

John interrupted to shake hands with Ben, "Good to see you again. I'm going to see if Lindsey's all right. See you tomorrow in the office."

"Cheers old chap. Looking forward to it."

"So am I," said John over his shoulder.

Ben took his bicycle clips out of his pocket and put them on his trousers, "I'm OK Susan, really I am, and I'm really happy you and John are going to live there. I just don't want to face up to watching all the demolition. But I've had to cope with worse. It's times like these when it's bad, late at night when I have to go home. Never mind. It'll be all right when I get to Spain," he added cheerfully.

Susan gave him a hug and watched him ride off on his bike. She went back to the dining room to find Lindsey unloading mugs of coffee from a tray. "Here you are Sis," she said, seeming much livelier, "This'll wake you up ready for bed!"

"Talking of which," said Susan, "what time is it?"

"Half eleven," said John.

"All right," said Lindsey, "I can sleep in the spare room can't I?"

"Of course," said Susan, "Did you think you were going to drive somewhere in your condition?"

"No, but I'm only a little bit drunk."

"We all are a bit," said Susan kindly.

"I wouldn't mind a fag.... Omega. ... No I wouldn't, I don't smoke. See, it works, I told you. Listen, let me tell you something while we finish our coffees," she said, speaking very quickly. Adam taught me something very interesting. He can cure people of phobias and smoking and stuff but part of the treatment is self-hypnosis so when I want to have a fag I just say a word in my head that I wouldn't normally use. Most people use a Greek letter. I just say Omega and then I don't want a fag at all. I had to be sort of 'conditioned' by him first but now I can do it myself. Well, I asked him if you can hypnotise yourself to do anything, and he said 'yes, very nearly,' and that anybody can do it if they really want to. You can improve your memory, learn languages, get rid of driving test nerves..... anyway, I asked him if I could get inside someone else's body, and if someone could get inside mine."

"That coffee must be doing amazing things to you," said John.

"Don't laugh, I can do it! He showed me how. I told you he was wonderful didn't I?"

171

"I don't understand," said Susan.

"I don't mean actually get inside someone else, I mean know how they feel on the inside. OK I'll show you, both of you. Just pull your left sleeve up and with your right hand middle fingertip just very gently touch your arm between your elbow and your shoulder. Hardly touch the skin at all. Move your finger up towards your shoulder...... and back again. OK stop. Now I'm going to hypnotise you. Don't panic, you will be fully conscious of everything that's happening and you will be totally in control and can stop whenever you like. Just sit comfortably and listen to the sound of my voice. I'm going to count backwards slowly from five and when I get to one you will be completely relaxed and happy and ready for me to help you. Five, four, three, two. one... A few minutes ago you touched your arm. Remember how it felt. Try to imagine what each of you would feel when touched by the other person. It would feel exactly the same for them as for you wouldn't it? John, I want you to touch Susan's arm, very gently, just above the elbow and you will be able to feel everything she feels as you move your finger. .... Can you feel it.?"

"Oh yes! Definitely."

"And whereabouts do you feel it.?"

"On my own arm, in the same place."

"Right, take your hand away now. Susan, reach out and touch John's arm. Can you feel what John is feeling?"

"Yes! Very much. He feels tickling!"

"Now both of you touch each other's arms. What can you feel? You feel what it's like for them to be touched by you but can you also feel what the other one feels when touching you?"

"Yes! Yes!" they both said at once.

"We've nearly finished now."

"Oh," they said, obviously disappointed.

"Don't worry you will be able to do this again whenever you want, you just have to remember two things. All you have to do is say the word Lambda when you start and the word Delta when you stop. Now sit comfortably again. I'm going to count from one to five and when I say five you will be wide awake and relaxed and be able to remember everything that has happened. One, two, three, nearly there, four... and five."

"Wow!" said Susan, "That was amazing."

"Very impressive," said John, "You should do this sort of thing as a career."

Lindsey leant back in her chair, stretched her arms up as far as they would go and yawned, "All right, that will be a hundred quid each please. Pay me in the morning, I'm going to bed."

"Is that it?" asked John. He put out his hand and touched Susan's arm, "It doesn't work now."

Lindsey stopped and turned round at the bottom of the stairs, "Yes it does. All you have to do is say the trigger word before you start. By-ee."

"OK, let's go to bed. I'm really sleepy now," said John, getting up and standing behind Susan's chair.

"Could we give it one more go," asked Susan, "I'm only interested for scientific reasons."

"Of course you are. OK both together, after three."

"I feel a bit silly."

"Don't look at me then. Are you ready...one two three, Lambda!" they both said together. John bent down and kissed her on the back of the neck. "I felt that here!" he exclaimed, holding his neck.

"And I felt it on mine. But here mostly!" she said,

pointing to her lips. John sat down in the chair next to her. Slowly, inevitably, they leant towards each other. They kissed and closed their eyes. As they parted they hardly dared to open them again. When they did they saw amazement each other's faces. Lindsey called down the stairs, "Good night!"

"What? Oh, Good night," said John

"Sis, you're too much."

"I know. Good though, innit."

"Do you want to say the finish word now?" asked John."

"Um .... perhaps a bit later."

Chapter Eighteen

Editorial meeting

When John arrived at the Gazette next morning he could tell that it was not going to be an ordinary day at the office. The main clue to this was that it was only just nine o'clock and all the reporting staff were already sitting at their desks, something he had never seen before. "I'm not late am I?" he asked Dick East.

"Not at all, but the boss told me he wants the meeting to start as soon as everyone has arrived, which is now really." John could see through the glass walls of the inner office where the editor was already chatting to Dr. Salter and Ben Carter. When he saw John arrive he opened his door and beckoned everyone in, "Make yourselves comfortable everybody. There's no need for introductions because you've all met Dr. Gerald Salter and Ben Carter many times I'm sure, on the other hand our guests won't know all of your names so please identify yourselves when you ask questions.

Before I start I want you to understand why we are having this rather melodramatic meeting. It's because when you leave this room I don't want you talking to anyone about what you are going to hear today. Basically this is our story and I don't want it leaking out before we publish on Wednesday. I can't control everything you say and do but just be sensible. If you want to tell your wives or husbands that's OK, if you trust them that is, but not the rest of your families. If I see it gets into the national papers before Wednesday I shall sack you all!" He smiled as he sat on the corner of his desk. Next to him was a wooden easel with a white sheet hanging over it. In the middle of the desk was a smaller object, similarly covered. "Dr. Salter, he says we can call him Gerry, has been working on the Snook mystery for nearly two months now and he's making amazing progress. His team has come up with some startling two and three dimensional images of Abigail, that is her real name by the way, and Dick handed me these just two weeks ago," he held up a sheaf of papers, brown with age, "They were given to him by Walter Chindell, a solicitor in Chesham, who is a collector of old letters and records. Mr. Chindell had never heard the highwayman story but after seeing the article in February's Gazette he remembered seeing the name Snook and decided to take another look at these documents. I'm not going to read them out because it's in rather old fashioned language and it would take ages, but I have in my hand the official version of the events before and after the execution. By official version I mean that it has been written by Dick using evidence gathered by Gerry's team as well as a great deal of help from the solicitor. So here goes." He stood behind his desk so that he could be properly seen and heard, "I'll leave out the bit we know already about how Snook tried to spend a huge bank note in London and how he was eventually captured. I'll start with the day before his execution when he was held prisoner in The Swan public house in Boxmoor.

Abigail Shepherd was a servant in a large house near Hatfield. At one time she had been Snook's lover and had given birth to their son who was now four years old. Because of her lowly status and the absence of a father she had no choice but to place him in an orphanage in St. Albans. Snook was unaware of the existence of his son but during her visit she told him he was the father of her child.

They made a plan for Snook to escape, Abigail having the desperate hope that they could live together as a family. He escaped by simply walking past the gaoler wearing her cloak and pretending to be weeping uncontrollably. Abigail hid under the blankets on his bed but was soon discovered by the gaoler. She professed her innocence claiming that Snook had tried to strangle her and she had passed out. However the gaoler, William South, harassed her into admitting she was a party to the escape.

Staying at the inn was a rich and powerful merchant who was also a magistrate. His name was Paul Steelman who lived in a large house in Berkhamsted and had friends within the Post Office. He was taking a great deal of interest in the proceedings and was intending to be the eyes and ears of these friends at the execution the following day. The gaoler interrupted his breakfast to tell him what had happened and he took command of the situation.

Word came that Snook had been seen running along the newly completed Grand Junction Canal, as it was called then, and the gaoler and four men went after him. They thought he was hiding in one of the many canal boats and began searching them one by one without success. It is reported that the gaoler shouted to a small group of boat people, "I know he's here somewhere. Tell him we have his mistress in custody and she will be hung for aiding his escape unless he gives himself up."

Snook jumped down from a willow tree where he was hiding and gave himself up to the authorities. Back at The Swan he told Steelman that he had overpowered Abigail and she was not a willing participant in the escape but he was ignored. Steelman met with Abigail and told her that she was liable be hung for helping Snook to escape but now he was captured again he would see to it that she would not be charged with any crime. There was one condition, she would have to become his mistress. She very reluctantly agreed to his demands as long as she was allowed to take her son from the orphanage and she was provided with enough money for her and her child to live on.

She was permitted a last meeting with Snook that evening. She told him that she was not to be charged and would be able to provide for their son but without telling him how. He told her he deserved his punishment and would die happier knowing she was to be free woman. The gaoler listened to every word of their conversation and reports that this is when Snook handed her the St. Christopher medal after telling her that he had worn it every day since she gave it to him. After an anguished parting the gaoler stopped her outside the cell. He told her that Steelman wanted her to visit him in his bedroom. He also warned her that he had overheard the so-called justice of the peace saying he had no intention of paying any money "to her or her bastard son" and that after he'd had his way with her he was going make sure she was arrested. She thanked the gaoler and said she was going home, instead of which she went into the kitchen and took away a large knife. On entering Steelman's room she tried to stab him but he fought her off. He was too strong for her. In one brief moment she realised her position was hopeless; she had lost her lover, she would never be able to help her son and was now in the power of this deceitful monster. As he strode towards her she held the knife to her chest and dropped face down on the floor with the full weight of her body falling on the blade. At the same moment the gaoler appeared at the open doorway.

"You saw it, didn't you?" exclaimed the merchant, "She must be mad, crazed with grief or something!"

They hid the body in his room until the day after the execution when the noble citizens of Hemel Hempstead provided a coffin for Snook who had been buried without one. Steelman paid the gaoler well and instructed him that the highwayman's body was not to be dug up and the poor girl was put in the coffin instead. The gaoler records that it was he who put the St. Christopher medal in her hand. The clergyman and the small group of people at the burial had no idea who they were putting into the ground."

The editor paused for another drink of water,

"What I have just read to you has been slightly 'dramatised for radio' as they say on the BBC. But it is pretty much all true. The information comes from two separate sources," he held up the old brown papers again, "the main one being William South, the gaoler who wrote down an account of the events that he experienced first-hand including the appalling behaviour of Steelman towards a vulnerable young woman. He left his writings with his son with instructions for him to make them available to the authorities after his death. I think it is fair to assume that he wanted Steelman to get his just desserts but feared the consequences of his own part in the business. It didn't quite work out as planned because the envelope containing his story was never opened for some reason and when it eventually came into the hands of our solicitor friend the seal was still unbroken.

Mr. Chindell has a brother Joseph who is another solicitor in Berkhamsted. Chindells have been solicitors in this area for more than two centuries and they never throw anything away, apparently. He asked brother Joseph to search his records and he discovered the last will and testament of Paul Steelman. This ignoble magistrate had no dependants and we can only suppose that he must have developed some kind of remorse, or thought he could buy his way into heaven, or way out of hell, because he left all his possessions to Charles Shepherd, the son of Abigail and Snook. The orphanage log records that a young man with that name left their establishment after inheriting a considerable fortune. He emigrated to America not long after the war of independence and did very well for himself. His descendants now own large parts of New Jersey.

That's me finished for a bit. I just want to add that our circulation rose quite a bit last week with the start of Hemel Spectacular but next Wednesday we should see a steep climb in the sales figures."

He sat down before asking Dr. Salter if he had anything to add, "Not very much really. Just to say that we have permission to re-start excavations in two weeks' time..... Yes, you have a question?"

"I'm Bill Porter," said a very young man with curly hair and thick glasses, "How hopeful are you that you will find Snook's body this time?"

"Porter the reporter! I like that. Sorry, you must have heard that hundreds of times. Very hopeful is the answer. The original grave is still open from when we were last at the dig and covered by some boards. That's where we will start. It seems extremely likely that the gaoler re-dug the grave in secret and left Snook's body at the bottom under a small amount of earth. Back in February none of us thought of digging any deeper but now I'm very confident we only need to dig only a few more feet to find him," he looked round at his audience,

"Any more questions? No?....Yes, Mr. Porter."

"How far have you got with the reconstruction of Abigail's face?"

"Ah. This is where we do some unveiling," he strode over to the desk and uncovered the round object which was a clay bust of a young woman with fairly ordinary but well-proportioned features. Even so this caused quite a sensation. John took some photographs with Dr. Salter and Ben standing behind it, "I think it's a pretty impressive piece of reconstruction but without hair I think it doesn't really do her justice. On the other hand," he said approaching the easel, "our artist is convinced this is pretty accurate impression of what she looked like." He carefully lifted up the sheet. This caused a few gasps amongst his audience. John, who was taking photographs of Dr. Salter in the act of unveiling, suddenly stopped what he was doing and sat down in a chair as if transfixed by what he saw.

It was a painting of a young woman, not peering directly out of the picture but slightly to her right and looking down. This semi-profile had enabled the artist to present a more believable likeness than the usual full-face view usually seen in police Identi-kit pictures. This position had very cleverly been chosen by the painter so that only a small part of the eyes could be seen, the actual colour being unknown. Unlike the clay likeness this one clearly showed someone who was very beautiful. Partially tucked under her white linen cap was a profusion of straight blond hair.

Chapter Nineteen

Revelation

"You're not going to say she looked like me are you?" said Susan to John later that evening in Herbert Street.

"No. She didn't, this is going to sound silly, but I really felt that I knew her. I don't mean someone like her, I mean Abigail herself. Ever since I first saw her skeleton I felt something, some kind of connection. I put it down to my imagination and my strong emotions after meeting you. Anyway let me finish telling you what else happened.

The meeting finished very soon after the unveiling and all the staff shuffled off back to their desks. I was still sitting in my chair, mesmerised by the painting, but woke out of my daydream because I heard the editor close his door, 'Sorry, I was miles away,' I said and got up to leave as well.

'No. You'd better sit down again,' he said as he and Dr. Salter and Ben pulled up some chairs and sat opposite me.

'Wait a minute,' I said, 'this is a bit like when the consultant has some bad news!'

'No no,' said Ben, 'It's a bit unbelievable and extremely interesting but there's nothing bad about it.'

Dr. Salter produced a print-out of an e-mail, 'Are you sitting comfortably?' He obviously saw that I wasn't and that I was actually getting a bit irritated so he come straight out with it, 'We have been in touch with various record offices in New Jersey and we can say with absolute certainty that you are related, albeit distantly, with both Snook and Abigail. You are in fact the great, great, great, great, great, grandson of Charles Shepherd.'

'I don't believe you,' I said looking from one to another as they all grinned back at me like Cheshire Cats, 'Yes I do, you wouldn't shoot me a line like that.'

'Yes it's true,' said the doctor, 'Of course there are a great many other young men and women who are alive and descendants of Charles Shepherd. Your DNA must be pretty much watered down but I'm sure it could be proved with the latest technology. It's a bit like being fiftieth in line to the throne so I don't suppose you are likely to inherit large parts of New Jersey.'

"Then I remembered who the painting reminded me of," said John to Susan, opening his lap-top computer, "just a minute - here she is," they were looking at a photograph of a painting in an oval frame, a picture of a young woman in semi-profile but looking to her left, "Now compare her with this picture I took of Abigail's painting this morning. Now if I just flip the image over so they are both facing the same way...."

"Oh my God, it's her! Who is she?"

"She was my great, great, grandmother. I knew a bit about her already, and my great, great, grandfather who was Herbert George Street. Lots of male Streets had Herbert in their name somewhere. My father was Michael John Herbert Street. Never mind all that, my great, great, grandmother's maiden name was Shepherd, Emily Shepherd. She ran away from her wealthy New Jersey family and lived on her own in Liverpool, a bold thing for a young woman to do in those days, and found employment as a secretary with great, great, grandfather Herbert. In amazingly unfashionable haste they got married. After the very quiet wedding they decided to pay a surprise visit to Emily's family in America. They sent a telegram to warn her parents of their intentions and marital status but received a reply telling them not to come, 'Never darken our door....' that sort of thing. Funnily enough, I mean strange, not funny, they had bought tickets to travel to New York on the Titanic but managed to sell them again at a good price. I say strange because if they had gone I would probably not be here. There you go. You might never have met me!"

"Good old Emily and Herbert. They sound interesting people. Definitely not drippy."

"But isn't that strange, me feeling sad about Abigail I mean. Mind you I would have felt sorry for her anyway I suppose."

"Ben warned us it would be a sad story but it has a happy ....happi- er ending, I suppose, with their son's life, and all the way down to you."

"Wow! I belong to the criminal classes."

"I always thought there was something dodgy about you."

"The editor wants to know if he can put my bit in the story. I wouldn't have thought it was that important but I suppose it brings in a bit of present day human interest," he looked at Susan, "I said I would ask you."

"I don't mind. I'm not so bothered about avoiding publicity now. Lindsey and I are going to pack in working for Zoldini."

"Really?"

"Yes, for two reasons. Firstly …. um, don't worry but I thought I missed my period this month, something that's never happened to me before. But don't panic, false alarm. It made me think, though. First of all I was thinking 'Oh my God that's a bit quick!' then when it started again I was a tiny bit sad. And then I thought if we are going to start a family it's probably not a suitable career for a mum to be a magician's assistant. It's been good money but I think it's time to pack it in now. I had a word with Lindsey this morning and she said she was just about to tell me that she has decided to sell her shop and business to the Jewish fashion king and move to Australia."

"Is Adam White going with her?"

"I don't think so. She told me this morning she's changed her mind about him."

"What about the most wonderful professional man on earth - and she had to marry him?"

"I hope you've begun to realise by now that Lindsey is somewhat changeable in her desires and intentions."

"No! That doesn't sound like your sister!"

"Oh, she's not completely gone off him. She told me that she still thinks he's wonderful but he wouldn't suit her long term. Anyway Zoldini will be furious but he's paid us for the last stunt so we are free to do what we want. Our contracts still prevent us talking about his tricks but that's not a problem," she sat on his lap and put her arms round his neck, "So are you still interested in starting a family? In which case what's your favourite word?"

"Yes, of course, but can we stretch 'now' a bit so we can see a bit of the world - have some fun."

"All right, we'll have a honeymoon while the architect draws up plans for the new house. Then we'll come back, build the house then have a baby."

185

"OK, scary stuff, very exciting. Wait a minute, honeymoon? Are we talking about getting married?"

"Oh, I can't be bothered with all that now. We'll do that later and have the reception in our new home."

"Like it. Like it."

"So what about your other woman, Abigail? What are you going to say to your editor about going public with your dodgy relatives?"

"I'm going to tell him no. He said he wouldn't mind and that it's not important. I just feel she needs a bit of respect in all this, from me at least. Do you think I'm a bit soft?"

"No. I don't. Do you?"

"No."

"Good."

"I love you."

"You better had."

Chapter Twenty

Nemesis Meeting

The following Tuesday John was in the Gazette office listening to Dick East,

"Saturday is the finale of Hemel Spectacular but we want some photographs for tomorrow's paper - preview shots of the new boating lake in the town centre. How much do you know about it?"

"I've seen the lake in the Water Gardens and the scale model of the Palace of Westminster and it's Big Ben clock tower. It's huge, it must be four metres high at least."

"It's going to be a permanent feature after Hemel Spectacular is finished. The clock is in full working order complete with Westminster chimes. I think it's actually quite good compared with the latest piece of town sculpture."

"Oh yes, Henry the Eighth. Why would anyone want to put a up a statue of him? He was a monster as far as I remember from school."

"It was our dear mayor's idea. We're still trying find out from the council how much it cost. Henry is supposed to have a sort of connection with the town because he granted some kind of market charter. Never mind all that. On Saturday councillor Mallacott and other dignitaries will sail across the lake in a flotilla of pleasure boats while on the bank a small orchestra will play Handel's Water Music. She will announce the end of Hemel Spectacular fortnight and just after the chimes of Big Ben she will declare the boating lake open and release loads of balloons. That's about it.

But for today's picture she is going to pose for us in front of Big Ben for a shot of her with the hands of the clock pointing to twelve. While you're there can you see if there's anything else worth a picture. I think they are delivering the boats this morning."

"I've taken a few shots already."

"I know. I love the one with the Palace of Westminster reflected upside down in the water. We've already placed that on the front page."

* * *

"Good morning Mr. Street," said Daphne Mallacott, without smiling. She gave John one of her 'wet fish hand shakes' as Dick East described them. "It was unforgivable of the Gazette to use those photographs of the accident with the statue. I have sent a letter of complaint to your editor but as yet I have had no reply. However I realise that you were only doing what you are paid to do so we'll let that pass. I only hope you can make a better job of it this morning. What would you like me to do?"

"Just stand where you are, please, just looking to your left."

"That's not my best side."

"OK then. Stand over there and look to your right."

"I don't like you having the camera down there. You'll make me look as if I have double chins."

"I'm sorry but I have to look up at you to get the clock tower in the background. It'll be all right if you lift your chin up ....."

"Yes, yes. Just hurry up will you."

"You'll have to wait thirty seconds because I want both hands at twelve." John wanted to ask her to wipe the lipstick off her teeth but decided against it, "There we go. All done. .... That's a shame, I was expecting to hear the chimes."

"They won't be switched on until just before the ceremony on Saturday. You should know that," she said, turning her back and walking away, "doesn't your paper tell you anything?"

John spotted a man with huge waders up to his chest pulling five paddle boats towards an anchor post in the middle of the lake where five more were already moored. As he took pictures of him he was reminded of a picture he had once seen in a Gulliver's Travels book.

Meanwhile, Ben Carter had just been putting some cheques in the bank and was walking and pushing his bicycle over a footbridge near the lake. Too late he spotted Daphne Mallacott on the far side of the bridge. They both stopped and stood quite still for a moment, the mayor looking at him with half-closed eyes. Ben turned round to find another way home.

"Mr. Carter," said the mayor, "Have you got a minute? I've been meaning to speak to you for some time." Ben stopped at his end of the bridge forcing his enemy to walk towards him if she wanted to continue the conversation. This she did. They stood facing each other on Ben's end of the bridge. He said nothing. "It's about your property Mr. Carter."

Silence.

"My company is prepared to make you a very reasonable offer for your piece of land."

Still Ben said nothing.

"Do you understand what I'm saying?

"Yes."

"Well?"

"It's not for sale."

"What do you mean? You'll have to sell it. You can't live there now."

"That's right. Thanks to you."

"The decision to demolish was made by a committee, not by me."

Silence.

"Well."

"Well what?"

"Aren't you interested in what my offer might be?"

"No."

"Why not."

"It's already sold."

"What! It can't be. There's been no 'For Sale' sign up and nothing in the estate agents' advertisements."

"I sold it privately."

"Who to?"

"A friend."

"That's madness. Whatever this friend is paying you I'm sure I can offer you more, and I will if you will listen to reason. I had great plans for that site."

"Well not any more you don't."

"But why? I don't understand?"

"Yes it must be difficult for people like you...."

"What do you 'mean people like me'?" she said in red-faced anger. By now a small group of people had gathered. They had been trying to cross over the bridge.

"People like you," said Ben loudly, "don't seem to be able to understand that there are more valuable things in life than money. Now get out of my way I'm going home." He pushed passed her and so did ten irritated people who followed right behind him.

Ben was pushing his bicycle through the garden on the other side of the bridge when he met John walking back to the Gazette office.

"You OK Ben? You look very serious."

"I've just been having an unpleasant talk with hundred and forty four."

"What?"

"Mrs. Mallacott. They call her that because she's gross."

"I've just photographed her by the new boating lake. She seemed more obnoxious than usual this morning."

"You should see her at a planning meeting, she's vicious."

"Is there a Mr. Mallacott?"

"You mean Geoff. Poor old sod. He became an alcoholic years ago. I know it's supposed to be an illness but with him it's controlled and self-inflicted oblivion. I'd have done the same I'm sure."

"You off to your place now?" He avoided the word 'home.'

"Such as it is. I'll have to move out before Friday, "I'm putting things in a heap ready for my son to put in the back of his car. I'm going to stay with him till I go to Spain. I'm only taking a few bits, clothes and stuff. I've already hidden the stove and solar panels in the woods for you and Susan. By the way, good news! I've managed to save the dam! Or rather I checked with my solicitor who says that it's not any part of the condemned dwelling so it can stay."

"Well done. I'm so pleased, and I know Susan will be over the moon."

"Give us a shout if you want some help."

"Thanks."

Ben arrived at his home to find some men standing on the brick road with a bulldozer, and a lorry with CROUCHER DEMOLITON written on its side. Leaning against the front wheel of the lorry was a fat middle-aged man with dyed blond hair and with his stomach imprisoned in the top of his trousers by a wide leather belt. Two German Shepherd dogs sat by his feet. As he drew near Ben could hear him instructing his men to attach a steel cable to the trunk of a tall beech tree.

"We'll give it a pull with the 'dozer and if it doesn't come down we'll get the chain saws on it."

"Excuse, me. Are you Mr. Croucher?"

"I am. You must be Mr. Carter. We haven't met. You weren't here when we cleared the first trees away. What can I do for you?"

"You aren't supposed to start work yet."

"Not on your land, no, but we are just getting rid of that tree so we can start first thing Friday morning." One of the dogs growled quietly while the other sniffed at Ben's trousers.

"That tree is on my land and there's a preservation order on it." Much as he tried Ben couldn't help looking at the thick tufts of hair sticking out of the man's nostrils.

"Our vehicles aren't on your land up here and nobody's said anything to me about keeping the tree so it's going, right?"

"I've said it."

"Look mate. Get on to your lawyer if you want. By the time he's got round to writing us a letter we'll be finished here and gone, so just keep out of the way." He spat on the ground, turned his back and walked towards the bulldozer.

Ben laid his bicycle down on the ground out of earshot and dialled 999 on his phone, "Police please..... Thank you. Ah yes. My name is Ben Carter. I'm at my property to the north of Hemel Hempstead. I have intruders on the premises committing criminal damage. You can't miss it... less than a mile out of town on the right hand side of the road. Yes, I'll be here waiting. No, I'm not under threat, just the property." He sat down to watch the men as one of them climbed up to a fork in the tree and pulled the steel cable after him. It took all four of them to feed it between the branches and down to the ground again. There was a hook on each end of the cable and these they attached to the rear of the bulldozer. The men stood back as their boss climbed into the cab and started the engine. Ben Carter quickly but calmly went and stood right in front of the bulldozer while Colin Croucher revved up the engine and sounded the vehicle's klaxon horn. The dogs were snarling at Ben's feet when the police car arrived with siren and lights flashing. The two officers ordered Croucher to switch off his engine while Ben explained the situation. The two officers then approached the demolition team. Ben watched Croucher pointing first at the tree and at the house and then at the tree again, John arrived, camera in hand and taking photographs. One of the policemen ran up to him, "Would you mind telling me what you are doing?"

"I'm from the Gazette. We picked this up from the your press office," said John as he continued taking pictures.

"I'm telling you to stop what you are doing and leave immediately. Have you any kind of identification on you?"

John showed him his press card and said politely, "I

don't want to cause any hassle but I am standing on a public highway and I'm not intruding because the tree and everything else is in full public view."

"You are obstructing my investigation."

"I don't think I am. Are you going to arrest me?"

The policeman's eyes glazed over slightly as he was thinking what to do, "No. But I'm entitled to confiscate your camera for evidence."

Ben coughed, "Excuse me officer, I know this gentleman. He's here at my invitation. Can I just have a word with him?" He took John to one side, "Look mate, don't let him take your camera. I know he's in the wrong but if he takes it he'll empty all the images out of spite. That what they did with me last time they got all nasty. Why don't you go and sit on the veranda till they've gone. You can take what pictures you like from there and I could do with a witness."

"OK sure," said John as he wandered off.

"Sorry about that, officer. He's very young and new to the job. What's going to happen here?" The other policeman joined them, "The bloke with the bulldozer has agreed to stop work until we find out who owns the tree and whether they are allowed to be working here."

"This land away from the road is mine. There is also a preservation order on the tree. You only need to check that with the council."

"Are they allowed to work here?"

"Not on my land till Friday morning, and they can't touch the tree even then. They can do what they like by the road here where we're standing."

"All right. If they haven't got any paperwork giving them permission I'll tell them to leave. It's up to you to contact the council about the tree. It's a civil matter." After a few words with Croucher the police walked to their car.

The bulldozer and lorry were driven a short distance away and parked on the grass verge of the main road. The men piled into a battered four wheel drive estate car, all except Croucher who strode down, accompanied by his dogs, to where Ben and John sat on the veranda.

"You shouldn't have done that Carter, I'm not the sort of bloke you want to get on the wrong side of. And you," he said, waving his fist at John, "those photographs had better not appear in the paper. Do you understand?"

"Perfectly," said John, picking up his camera and flashing it in Croucher's face, "How about a nice smile for the readers."

"Why you little prick! I'll do for you."

John stood up, "Careful Mr. Croucher," the police are parked up by the road watching your every move." Croucher slowly turned and looked over his shoulder.

"Why don't we all give them a cheery wave," said Ben as he and John did just that.

Croucher shouted over his shoulder as he marched back to his estate car, "You just wait till Friday, then we'll see …. then we'll see!" He got in, slammed the door, spat through the window and roared away up the brick roadway.

"Well done you," said John.

"Thanks mate," said Ben.

"Are you going to be all right on Friday?"

"I won't be here then. I'm going to Whipsnade Zoo with the grandchildren and on Saturday I'm not going on the site. I'm going to watch them finish from up there on the hill. Susan said she would come and sit with me. She's good like that."

"I know she is. I'll be around as well if you want me."

"Thanks mate."

Chapter Twenty One

Lindsey Says Goodbye

It was Thursday morning at Herbert Street and John had overslept soundly as befitted the usual plan for his regular day off. But now it was ten o'clock and his phone rang.

"Hello Susan."

"Aaah, you sound all sleepy, sweetheart."

"No..... wide awake," he said, lying and yawning at the same time.

Susan adopted her nasal accent that she used to warn people she wanted something, "Can you do me an enormous favour?"

"What?"

"It's Lindsey. She's on her way to Australia."

"Already? She doesn't hang about does she."

"I'm quite upset about it really. Sometimes she just doesn't think about how other people might feel but it would have been nice for us to say good-bye or give her a lift to the airport or something. You know people sometimes say they hate good-byes, well Lindsey really hates them. I think she just finds the emotion of parting too much for her. She did manage to phone me at least.

She got a cancellation ticket. She's not emigrating or anything - not yet anyway. Do you remember I said my brother Andrew was in Perth? She's going to stay with him for a while."

"How long for?"

"Oh I don't know! She's done this lots of times in her life. Not emigrated, but left home or left the country never to return. When she was six years old and being naughty she would be sent to her room and then Mum or Dad would catch her walking down the road dragging a suitcase. Can you imagine that?"

"Oh yes, easily."

"She says she's thinking of opening a dress shop and is hoping Andrew will help her find one she can buy, on the other hand she might be back next month."

"What do you want me to do?"

"She's still at Heathrow airport. Her flight's been delayed so she'll be there another five hours. She forgot to pick up some money-transfers or something from Barclay's Bank in Barnet. Could you pick them up and take them to her? I'll pay for the petrol."

"No you won't," said John amiably, "You'll just have to be in my debt."

"And how do I repay you?"

"Don't worry I'll think of something."

"You're an angel."

"I know."

"The bank will be OK if you have some identification. Lindsey is at Terminal Three, the 0032 Quantas flight to Sydney. Give her my love won't you."

"Of course, but I don't much like the way she's treating you - us."

John marched in through the automatic sliding glass doors and into the Terminal Three passenger concourse. He followed the signs to the Quantas check-in desks where there were four motionless queues of people. Some were sitting on the floor while single limp figures guarded bags and suitcases for their partners or relatives.

As John arrived many of these people stirred into life as uniformed women and men appeared at the check-in desks and began to switch on lights. He dialled Lindsey's number on his mobile phone but it was engaged. He walked slowly along the queues without success. '*I would have thought she would be easy to find. Maybe she's dressed as a nun or a kangaroo or something.*' He stopped beside a young woman sitting on a huge suitcase reading a story book to a small boy. She had straight bobbed blond hair which just reached her shoulders and wore a dark green tailored jacket and skirt. People in the queue were beginning to move so John dialled Lindsey's number again.

"Hello John, I'm near the check-in desks," said the young woman in the green suit, turning round, "Ah, there you are ..... just a minute." The small boy's mother collected her son and thanked Lindsey for her kindness.

"I hardly recognised you," said John, handing her the parcel, "I've never seen you looking so smart and with hardly any make-up."

"Thank you so much for getting these for me. Were they OK at the bank?"

"They just looked at my driving licence. Parking was a nightmare though." The queue moved forward a little so John dragged her suitcase for a couple of metres, "What have you got in here, a pair of anvils?"

"Look, don't stay. It'll cost you a bomb for car parking."

"I'm all right. I bought an hour's worth which is the cheapest rate anyway. I'll just stay till you're checked in, just in case ..... you know."

"In case I bugger something else up."

It seemed to John that Lindsey seemed vulnerable suddenly, something else he had not experienced before, but still he said, "You seem to know what you're doing, as always."

"Is that what you think?"

"I hope so. You're taking quite a big leap into the unknown, is that right?"

"I've done it before, besides it won't be that much into the unknown. I've got to see if I can make a living first, then I'll buy a shop like I had in Barnet, or I might buy a house and take a lease out on a shop. I dunno really. I'm going to have to suck it and see."

They arrived at the desk and Lindsey checked-in her bag and herself without mishap apart from the man behind the desk asking if they were travelling together. This resulted in a barely noticeable pause before Lindsey said, "No. It's just me," without looking at John. Then, when she was armed with her boarding pass and relieved of her suitcase, she said, "I've got ages before I have to go through to departures. Can I buy you a coffee?"

John glanced up at the huge clock in the middle of the hall, "OK, I've still got half an hour." When they were sitting down he said, "I'm sure you'll be all right but I just wish someone was going with you. By the way, why did you give up on your hypnotherapist?" He looked up at Lindsey and was shocked to see her purse her lips before huge tears ran down her cheeks. John passed her the little metal box with paper napkins in. She grabbed a handful and dabbed her eyes and cheeks and chin and blew her nose, "I'm sorry, this is so silly. You weren't meant to see this. I thought I was strong enough. I was sure I could hide it all." She took a deep breath followed by a massive sigh and two huge sobs. She looked at John with moist red eyes "I'm fine now, honestly."

"Oh sure, and I'm the Queen of Sheba!"

"All right here it is. There is no Adam White, well, there is and he's a hypnotherapist and he stopped me smoking, but it's not him I've got a crush on …..........it's you! ......I just couldn't bring myself to tell you. How could I? I shouldn't be telling you now, I suppose, only it doesn't matter so much if I'm not going to be around, does it? Did you have any idea? Say something for Christ's sake!"

"Just give me a second," said John, rubbing his eyebrows with his knuckles and then blowing his nose on some paper napkins, "they're going to charge us for these if we're not careful." He looked at Lindsey very briefly then began screwing up the napkins into a tight ball. After about twenty seconds, which seemed a lot longer for Lindsey, he began speaking slowly and deliberately, "Yes, I'm sure I was aware of what you felt, but I think I was putting it out of my mind and I had the feeling that you were doing the same, or trying to at least. Am I right?"

"Yes."

"And you nearly came out with it when we were having dinner didn't you?"

"It's very dangerous for me when I drink too much."

"Have you told Susan?"

"I haven't, but she knows, I can tell."

"Oh."

"Don't worry. There's nothing wrong with anything here. You and Susan are deeply in love with each other, no question. It's obvious to anyone who sees you together.

I know my sister and she has been like someone who's won the lottery jackpot ever since she met you. Maybe that's the problem. I'm so close to her that it would be impossible for me not to like you. The problem is how strong my feelings are."

"You're not going away because of me are you?"

"Pretty much, yes."

"Now I feel really rotten."

"Good! No.... You know I don't mean that."

"Yes."

Silence, then John spoke again, "Maybe if I had an identical twin that would have solved the problem."

"Maybe. Twins have married twins lots of times. But I don't think so really. Women choose partners for who they are more than what they look like. So unless he had the same personality as yours I wouldn't be interested, and if he had it would be a nightmare. Imagine if I had the same personality as Susan!"

"No, no! I don't even want to think about that."

They were both smiling now, a bit.

"Airports aren't designed for emotional outpourings are they. Perhaps the architects don't want anything to get in the way of moving people about efficiently. God, I bet I look a mess. Good job I'm not wearing make-up. It'd be all over my face by now."

"I like you without it. You look all young and clean."

"Thank you."

"I don't mind a bit of mascara on a model but most people don't need all this stuff they sell with lies like, anti-aging and contains Ziggurat B with extra bicycle clips," Lindsey laughed, "There you go. You feeling a bit better?"

"A bit."

"I'm glad you said it."

"Are you sure? I am too then."

"I was convinced I was in love with this girl eight years ago when I was nineteen. She was one of our group of friends that had been together since we were children, but I always thought she was too good for me. University happened and we all drifted apart. She married a good-looking Cambridge graduate and has three children. Last year one of my mates told me how much this girl wanted me and he was amazed that neither of us said anything."

"And?"

"And nothing. Life goes on. She's happy. I'm happy. You're going to be happy. Do you believe that?"

"Yes. But it still hurts now. You're the 'now' expert. When does it become a different 'now' when I'm happy too?"

"Sooner than you think, I hope. I mean that, and make sure you tell me when, please. I will be really happy as well."

"Thank you for staying with me," she stood up suddenly. "I'm going now. I can do this. Just don't say good-bye and don't touch me or I'll disintegrate." John stood up and felt useless as she picked up her bag and walked over to the departure gate. He watched as she handed over her passport and boarding card for inspection without looking back. He caught a glimpse of her beyond the gate chatting to another passenger. Just before she disappeared altogether he caught sight of her behind a plate glass partition. She had her hands on the glass as she tried to peer through. He waved but he was sure she couldn't see him.

He phoned Susan, "Mission accomplished. She's on her way with everything she needs."

"Was she all right?"

"Not really. Floods of tears but I made her smile a bit. …. I'm going to miss her."

"Me too. You know she loves you."

"Yes. She said as much."

"Well she can't have you."

"She knows that."

"And you?"

"I know that too."

"Good."

"Anyway you're too much for me so why would I want anyone else?"

"Come home this minute."

"Yes milady."

He put his car park ticket into the machine. It was just out of time so he paid the extra cost.

Chapter Twenty Two

Big Ben

Saturday morning started with a few late April showers which stopped in time for the multi-coloured strings of triangular plastic flags to be hung around the boating lake. Red, white and blue bunting adorned the model of the Palace of Westminster and also decorated the large landing stage just in front of it. Directly opposite, on the south side of the lake near the Riverside shopping centre, ten three-metre long paddle boats waited in their moorings to carry the mayor and her party around the lake before the opening ceremony. Waterhouse Street, on the east side, was closed for the occasion and had tiered seating on the waterside pavement. These seats were filling up fast as children and adults arrived and stationed themselves all around the lake. Thousands of white helium filled balloons were confined under a large net in the middle of the water. It was tied to the post where the boats were tethered the night before. A platform had been erected on the west side for members of the Dacorum Symphony Orchestra who were already arriving and unpacking their instruments. The time, shown clearly on the dial of the still silent Big Ben tower, was eleven o'clock. Fifteen minutes later John arrived on the scene and was met by a familiar face.

"Greetings dear boy, always happy to see a fellow sufferer again." It was the toastmaster that he had met in the marquee two weeks ago. This time he was dressed as the town crier but had replaced his hand bell with a powerful megaphone, "Do you know the programme?"

"I think so. If you could tell me when things happen that would be very helpful."

"Eleven twenty five, mayor and party arrive and get in the boats. Eleven thirty they sail across to the landing stage by Big Ben. Eleven forty, mayor makes speech, then goes by boat to the middle of the lake. Eleven fifty eight -ish I get the crowd to do a count down from ten. Then, hopefully the Big Ben clock starts its Westminster chimes and at the first stroke of twelve the mayor releases the balloons......

......Then we all go home."

"Thank you. That helps me a lot," said John as he caught sight of Dick East, Bill Porter and a photographer walking round the edge of the lake towards him.

"Morning," said Dick, with his usual broad grin.

"Hello," said John, "You always look as though you come to these events to get a laugh out of them."

"Of course. Why else would I do the job? I wouldn't want to work for a living."

"Me neither."

"By the way this is Stan Cash. He's one of our staff photographers, not the one with appendicitis the one who was on holiday," he wandered off with Bill Porter leaving the photographers together.

"Hello" said Stan, "I've heard all about you. I loved your shots of the mayor with the statue. Perhaps you're a jinx. Are you going make her boat sink or something this morning?"

"I'll do my best! So. Yes. If we're both covering this where do you want to be?"

"Dunno, don't care much."

"Well I fancy going up to the top of the shopping centre so I can get a shots of the general scene and then the procession with a long lens. And when they let the balloons go I can get them coming up towards the camera."

"OK, you go up and I'll stay down. I can't stand heights anyway."

"How's your colleague with the appendicitis?"

"He phoned in yesterday and said that it was a 'grumbling appendix' but he would still be off for another two weeks," he looked over his shoulder and then spoke quietly, "Strictly between ourselves you understand, he's not coming back."

"Is he really ill then?"

"No," he laughed, "I saw him at Watford Football Club last Saturday covering the match for the one of nationals. He's going freelance."

"Wow."

"I'm just telling you because there will be a job going here soon. The money's not much but if you were interested you'd stand a good chance. The editor thinks you're magic of course," he smiled, "I know you're crap but I won't tell anyone!"

"Thanks for that. I'd definitely be interested."

"OK, see you later."

Dick East drifted back again, "I wouldn't want to tell you chaps your job or anything but the balloons are quite important. They've all been labelled and paid for by the punters and there's a two hundred quid prize for the one that goes the furthest. Loads of kids will be holding them as well and they are going to let them go during the boat procession."

John walked across the road to the shopping centre and had a quick word with the manager of the largest department store who agreed to let him onto the roof as long as he went with a member of his staff.

From his superb vantage point he could see the whole of the lake and half a mile of the River Gade that fed it from the north. Down below him the mayor and her party were taking their time getting into the boats. About twenty Canada geese approached them like an armada and began to pester them for food. A section of the crowd began singing "Why are we waiting," so the orchestra began playing Handel's Water Music to drown their voices. John decided he had enough time to phone Susan to find out what was happening at the demolition site, "How you doing?" he asked, "It's all happening here but I've got a couple of minutes. I was wondering how Ben is bearing up."

"Oh, he's all right, considering. They've actually finished and carted everything away now. They didn't find the solar panels or the stove by the way. We're just waiting till Mallacott's brother leaves the site. Ben doesn't trust him. We're sitting near the top of Galley Hill so he doesn't realise we're watching everything he does."

John got some good shots of the boats as they snaked across the lake in single file with Daphne Mallacott providing plenty of 'royal waves' for the crowd. As they passed the grandstand seats all the children spontaneously let go of their balloons with the adults quickly following suit. Luckily for John the wind was in his direction so he had a wonderful close-up picture of the balloons with the whole lake beneath them. Because the boats began disembarking ahead of schedule he had half a mind to go down to ground level but decided against it and exchanged the wide-angle lens on his camera for a telescopic one. The orchestra went silent as the mayor walked across the landing stage to the microphone. There was an excellent sound system so John, whether he wanted to or not, could hear every word she uttered.

"Good morning ladies and gentlemen and children of course. That was a great privilege, just then, to be the first people to sail on this new boating lake. I hope you all manage to do the same very soon during this wonderful summer we are about to have.

I'm told that the boats will be available this afternoon, free of charge until five o'clock today. There is very likely to be a bit of a queue so you might want to come back later in the week. The hire fee will only be two pounds for half an hour. I would just like to congratulate, Keith Smythe..."

'no relation I hope,' thought John,

"…... who is standing beside me. As well as being a successful architect he is an expert model maker and has built, completely free of charge, this splendid replica of the Palace of Manchester..." she paused as Mr.Smythe whispered in her ear, "sorry, a slip of the tongue, I of course meant the Palace of Westminster or as it is perhaps better known to us, the Houses of Argument. In a few minutes I shall sail, or should I say paddle, single handed to the centre of the lake. There I shall wait to release the balloons just as Big Ben begins to strike twelve."

She tottered towards one of the boats which the town crier was holding steady for her. When she was seated he gently pushed the boat off while the orchestra played the

Hallelujah Chorus. Hemel Hempstead's first lady made a valiant effort to paddle her boat in a straight line but went in a complete circle back to the landing stage. After some helpful advice from the town crier she proceeded in a more or less straight line to the centre of the lake accompanied by the Canada geese honking in single file behind her.

"That was John," said Susan, "he was just asking what was going on here."

"That's nice of him," said Ben, "He's probably pretty busy right now."

From where they were sitting they could see Colin Croucher . He was standing with his hands on his hips next to his mechanical digger in the middle of the bare patch of ground which was once Ben's home. After half a minute he climbed into the cab and drove up to towards the entrance gate. The gate, along with a section of substantial fencing, had been put in place by the council to keep out anyone tempted to use the site for illegal dumping. Croucher didn't open the gate but climbed up it to look up and down the road. He seemed to be satisfied that he was unobserved so he climbed back into his digger, turned it round a drove back where he came from.

"What's he doing?" asked Ben. "He's bloody well up to something that's for sure."

Croucher drove over to the river and just to one side of the dam. From there he extended the arm of the digger so that it's bucket hooked onto the top of one of the steel shutters on the right hand side of the dam. He put the digger into reverse and began tugging at the shutter in an attempt to work it loose.

"Looks like he's trying to drain the water out," said Susan, "Why would he want to do that?"

"Because he's a nasty bit of work," said Ben, "Wait a minute! If he pulls that shutter out the whole lot will collapse!" He began running down the hill but stopped and watched in horror as his prediction came true. The rest of the steel shutters fell like dominoes and a huge wall of water shot out as if a giant bucket of water had been tipped over. It almost submerged Croucher and his digger before it rushed down the inadequate channel of the River Gade as fast as a speeding lorry. "You'd better phone John," shouted Ben, "He'll be able to warn the people at the lake! Don't call the police they'd never be ready in time."

"Damn! My battery's gone again," said Susan.

"And I've not brought my phone!" said Ben.

They looked around, but there was no-one. Ben started to run towards the nearest house he could see but stopped after a few minutes. He came walking back and as he met Susan he panted out, "No point. No point at all. The water will be there already."

"But what will happen to it after that?"

"It'll probably flatten out in the lake and whatever's left will tip into the canal at Two Waters."

They looked down towards the empty dam where a soaking wet Colin Croucher was kicking the side of his digger in a frantic rage.

"It's awful I know," said Susan, "but John and I will build another one I promise."

"I wonder what's happening in town," said Ben.

Daphne Mallacott managed to reach the centre of the lake and tied the boat up to the same post which held the massive balloon net. She rose to her feet.

"Probably not advisable to stand up, Madam Mayor,"

210

said the town crier through his megaphone. Madam Mayor waved in agreement and sat down again, "When you're ready just pull the iron ring off the hook and the balloons will come loose." He looked at his watch then pointed his megaphone at the grandstand seats, "It's countdown time. Are you ready, ten, nine, eight, seven, six, five, four, three, two, ONE!" The amplified Westminster chimes resonated from the replica Big Ben tower.

John was still on the roof of the shopping centre. He first became aware that something strange was happening when every goose, duck and seagull suddenly took off from the water. Immediately after, he noticed some feverish activity up the river from the lake. People were running to the left and right of the river and then he saw others were leaping out of the way of the rapidly approaching wall of water. He started waving madly at the town crier and pointing at the impending danger. By some miracle he spotted John's signal, saw what was coming down the river and began shooing the mayor's party along the landing stage towards safety. This was almost too late for some but these, luckily, only suffered from a severe soaking. The security man next to John had the presence of mind to radio down to his colleagues, some of whom had gone outside to watch the event. They managed to move some vulnerable people away from the water's edge.

Daphne Mallacott was still listening to the Westminster chimes and waiting for the first stroke of twelve. She was blissfully unaware of the approaching doom, mistaking the frantic gestures from the crowd as enthusiastic waving. She leant across from the front of the boat to the iron ring.

"DONGGGG!" She unhooked the ring.

"DONGGGG!" The boat rose vertically for two metres.

"DONGGGG !" The boat fell vertically for two metres.

"DONGGGG!" Mayor Mallacott stayed where she was suspended in the air, buoyed up by the thousands of helium balloons still trapped in the net.

"DONGGGG!" Mayor Mallacott rose to the occasion, or rather rose above the occasion as her shoes dropped from her feet into the water. Luckily she somehow managed to keep hold of her weighty handbag which prevented a too rapid ascent.

"DONGGG!" The balloons decided that this was just the right time to escape from the net and fly heavenwards.

"DONGGG!" The earth's gravitational force decided that this was also just the right time to recall the First Lady of Hemel Hempstead to her proper place on the surface of the planet.

"DONGGG!" Daphne Mallacott dropped into the water.

To the accompaniment of the remaining four chimes several boats were launched and raced as fast as possible towards the mayor who was now standing up to her ample waist in the water. She managed to catch her shoes as they floated by. With great difficulty, and with much loss of dignity, she allowed herself to be hoisted into one of the rescue boats which carried her back to the landing stage. The orchestra started playing soothing music which was almost drowned by the sound of police car sirens heading north on the main road out of town. The crowd gave the mayor a standing ovation for her gallant efforts, particularly the children who were hysterical with glee at what they had just witnessed. It had been one of those moments the details of which would be told and retold in the school playgrounds of Hemel Hempstead on Monday morning. It would mean utter misery for those children who WERE NOT THERE. As predicted by Ben Carter, the mini tsunami flattened itself quite considerably by the time it reached the far end of the lake and then poured itself into Grand Union Canal. By some miracle no one was seriously injured. John compared his photographs with those taken by Stan Cash and they both proudly showed the images to Dick East who, grinning as usual, said, "We're going to have a hell of a paper again this week."

John's telephone rang, it was Susan calling him from a public phone box on Galley Hill, "No we're all fine here," he said, "No one's been hurt as far as I can tell …….. No! That's incredible! Thanks for telling me…… OK . I'll see you and Ben in The Old Bell for a spot of lunch if you like. Bye." He looked at his companions, "You're not going to believe this. You know Colin Croucher, Mallacott's brother, the police found him and his mechanical digger up-river by the wreckage of Ben Carter's dam - and they've arrested him!"

Blissfully unaware of the latest turn of events Daphne Mallacott was being interviewed by the local radio reporter, "I've never seen so much water," she said as her voice was relayed over the loud speakers, "It was just like Viagra Falls!"

Epilogue

Colin Croucher was charged with criminal damage and endangering lives for which he received a two year custodial sentence. This was later reduced to a huge fine and he was ordered to do community service for eighteen months. He was also ordered to pay compensation enough to rebuild the dam. This was eventually done under the supervision of Susan and John who had an architect design a miniature replica of the Aswan dam in Egypt. It was constructed using reinforced concrete on the insistence of the local council to meet stringent safety standards.

Daphne Mallacott finished her year of office as mayor without further mishap. However her reputation suffered as a result of her brother's criminal convictions and she lost her deposit in the council elections the following year.

After completing the sale of his land to Susan, Ben Carter moved to Spain where he fulfilled his dream to teach painting and grow old ungracefully.

Lindsey started making dresses in Perth with her own shop and soon made enough money to employ a manager and dressmakers so she could be a stunt woman for Australian television and film makers. While doing this she met a six foot eight lifeguard called Steve Benson, and married him soon after their son was born. He was named John Herbert Benson.

Doctor Salter and his team began excavations again and found Snook's remains. As predicted they were less than a metre down from where Abigail was found. Plans to extend the by-pass were abandoned so that it became possible to arrange a re-burial. At the ceremony, attended by more than a hundred people, the couple were placed in the same grave and two headstones erected side by side.

John joined the staff of the Gazette. He sold his house in Herbert Street to buy half of Susan's land and help to pay for the building of their new home. Susan and he married at the register office in Hemel Hempstead old town. Ben Carter came over from Spain to give the bride away. Lindsey and Steve travelled right across the world to witness the marriage. They brought Susan's brother Andrew with them, as well as his partner Bruce, to be best men. They seized upon their roles with colourful enthusiasm and boundless wit. When the newlyweds came out of the register office they were greeted by the entire staff of the Gazette as well as that of Fenson's estate agents where Susan was still working, and, of course, 'Nell Gwyn' and Craig were there with copious amounts of confetti. Seven months later Susan gave birth to twins, not identical but very much alike. A boy and a girl, Benjamin Herbert and Emily Abigail, with Street for their surnames. They did think of giving them hyphenated surnames but Emily and Benjamin Street-Savage didn't sound quite right somehow.

The End.

Lightning Source UK Ltd.
Milton Keynes UK
UKOW031830220212

187769UK00001B/3/P